NOVEMBER KNIGHT

JUSTICE, MONTANA SERIES
- BOOK THREE -

DEBBI MIGIT

Scrivenings
PRESS
Quench your thirst for story.
www.ScriveningsPress.com

Published by Scrivenings Press LLC
15 Lucky Lane
Morrilton, Arkansas 72110
https://ScriveningsPress.com

Printed in the United States of America

Editors: Elena Hill and Susan Page Davis

Paperback ISBN 978-1-64917-345-4

eBook ISBN 978-1-64917-346-1

For my children, Alex, Ethan, and Kate. You are my very best blessings!

ACKNOWLEDGMENTS

Thank you to my cousin, Krista, for being my partner in (fictional) crime.

Thank you to Linda Fulkerson, Elena Hill, Susan Davis, and all of my friends in the Scrivenings Press family

PROLOGUE

Sierra

I pull my car into a parking spot at Selway Park on the outskirts of Dillon, Montana. The leaves of the aspen trees rustle in the November wind, reminding me that autumn is almost over, and winter is coming. But today is sunny, even if it's chilly, and I'm glad I agreed to meet Sophie here instead of on campus.

I was hesitant at first to join the Montana Mentors program, but just a few weeks with Sophie has settled my fears. At age twelve, she is bright and funny, with just a little bit of attitude. I understand. I've been developing my own attitude since beginning college two months ago. Nothing serious, just a restless urge for freedom.

On cue, my phone rings, and I see *Mom* on the caller ID. My fingers hover over the button. Should I answer? I love my mom —I really do. We've been alone since my dad was killed in Afghanistan eleven years ago. But I'm nearly twenty now, and it's time I get to make my own adventures.

I slide the phone into my pocket and climb out of the car, scanning the park for Sophie. She's sitting on a bench, her slender shoulders hunched against the breeze. Before I can call out to her, an SUV pulls up to the curb near her, and two women climb out. One is tall, wearing skin-tight black leggings with a leopard print jacket, red heels, and bright red lipstick. The other is younger and seems reluctant to follow.

My heart races as they approach Sophie, and I run flat out toward them. I'm on the varsity volleyball team at the University of Montana, and I'm suddenly thankful for those dreaded wind sprints Coach uses for torture. She calls it training, but hey, potato, potahto.

"Sophie!" My voice carries to the trio, and Sophie jumps up, only to be pushed onto the bench by the older woman.

I put on a burst of speed and nearly overshoot them. Grabbing the back of the bench, I stop my race and gasp, "Sophie, come with me. Right now."

Sophie tries to stand again, but the younger woman sits next to Sophie, holding her in place.

"Who are you? What do you want?" I demand.

A man approaches, and even at a distance, I can smell the acrid scent of garlic on his breath. At least he's safe from vampires.

"We just want Sophie, but since you crashed our party you're comin', too." Garlic Breath grabs Sophie's arm and hauls her up. "C'mon, Sophie Girl, you're gonna take a little ride with us," he says. Sophie swings around, her hand reaching for me, terror in her eyes.

"No, she is not." I say firmly. Well, as firmly as I can with whole-body tremors. I scan the park, looking for anyone to help us, but no one is around.

"Why?" Sophie's voice is steady, and I'm proud of her. "Who are you?"

"Well, ain't that the forty-six-thousand-dollar question," Garlic Breath cackles.

"Sixty-four," the first woman and I say at the same time.

"Huh?" Garlic Breath looks between the two of us.

"Never mind." She sighs.

"Anywho, my name ain't none of your business, little girl. Just know that your Uncle Travis has something that belongs to me. Something I want really bad. So, I figure I'll take something of his. Something to encourage him to give it back." While his tone seems almost friendly, I quickly look at his eyes, and a shudder passes down my spine. This man is dangerous.

"You'll have to find another way to negotiate with Travis," I say. "Sophie's not part of the deal."

"Now, I agree I have to change my plans just a little bit, seein' as you showed up unexpected like." Garlic Breath glares at the women. "Get 'em in the car."

"No!" Sophie and I struggle as the women grab us.

"Well, ain't it fortunate I remembered to bring my persuader along." All affability is gone as Garlic Breath pulls a gun and herds us toward the SUV. Sophie and I are shoved onto the filthy floor in the back while the older woman climbs into the driver's seat.

"Keys," Garlic Breath snaps.

"What?" I stare up at him, my heart racing.

"Give me your car keys." He speaks slowly like he's talking to a toddler.

I glare at him but toss my keys in his direction. He catches them in midair then passes them to the younger woman, who stands outside the SUV.

"Follow us," he commands tersely.

Garlic Breath settles into the front passenger seat and turns to point the gun in our direction. "Okay, girlies, here we go," he sings out. "Consider yourselves kidnapped."

1

Monday
November 11
2:00 p.m.

Jess

"Jess, this isn't smart." My best friend, Grace, is breathless as she tries to keep up with me. I shorten my steps, realizing my attempt at a casual stroll has morphed into a power walk.

"You're right," I agree. "I was walking too fast. We need to act normal, to avoid suspicion." Several college students are approaching on the sidewalk, and I grab Grace's arm, throw my head back, and laugh like she's said something hysterically funny.

To her credit, Grace goes along with the fake joke until the students pass, then abruptly stops laughing. "Yep, not suspicious at all." Her tone implies an eye roll. "I meant, it's not a good idea to be here, on this campus. Nick needs to investigate. He's the deputy sheriff, after all."

"*Hmm*," I answer, which translates into, "I hear you, but I'm ignoring your advice."

"You're ignoring my advice, aren't you?" Grace asks.

"*Hmm.*"

"Well, at least I can tell everyone I tried." The resignation in her sigh tugs at my conscience, and I try to reassure her. I've been eager to search for Sierra and am relieved that today is Veteran's Day and there's no school.

"It's just a little intelligence gathering. Sierra called Nick on Saturday and claimed someone had taken her. When he went to Missoula to search, he found out the police and FBI are investigating a trafficking ring operating near the campus. He can't be certain traffickers took Sierra, but it's a place to start."

"I'm confused," Grace says. "Why are we looking for clues in Dillon if Sierra is attending the University of Montana in Missoula?"

"Nick says Sierra volunteers at the Youth Challenge Program here at Montana Western twice a month. Her Missoula roommate, Gwen, thinks that's where she was going Friday afternoon. Sierra always stays on campus here with her friend Naomi when she's in Dillon."

"Sierra has a big heart if she volunteers two weekends a month to help at-risk kids," Grace says. "But you said she was skipping trips home and not answering calls. Why would she pull away from her family and friends?"

"I'm not sure," I reply. "Let's find her and ask."

As we turn a corner, a large brick building looms in front of us. I infuse my tone with surprise. "Hey, look. Magnus Hall. Naomi lives here."

"Shocking."

I frown at Grace's tone. While sarcasm is pretty much my default setting, Grace is very trusting and sweet. But over the past few months, my "adventures," as I call them, have sharpened Grace's edges more than a little. Great, I've broken my best friend.

"C'mon." Grace's genuine smile eases my conscience. "Let's check if Naomi is around."

I shake my head. "She's in Justice, being interviewed by Nick and Levi."

"How'd you know that?" Grace asks, then she laughs. "Never mind, stupid question."

"There are no stupid questions," I quote our French teacher, Madame Fellini.

Grace finishes the quote with a grin. "Only stupid accents."

For a moment I consider looking around Naomi's dorm room for any clues about Sierra but dismiss the idea. Normally, my philosophy is, 'what's a little B and E between friends.' But I've only met Naomi once and I'm not sure our relationship has reached that level yet.

"C'mon." I tug Grace's arm and turn us back toward the student parking lot, where I parked my sister's car. "I was wrong to think we'd find Sierra on campus. She claimed someone grabbed her. Maybe she's in another state by now." I'm surprised when my voice cracks with those last words.

We climb into Sly's Honda and sit in silence for a minute, then Grace says, "I'm scared."

"Me too."

"Does Nick have any clues at all?" Desperation laces her words.

Deputy Sheriff Nick McBride is Sierra's cousin, and the one she called Saturday. He's also Sly's boyfriend, while his younger brother, Cole, is my boyfriend. I guess we like to keep things in the family.

Sierra had called Nick during a family gathering, which included the entire McBride and Thomas clans. Well, the McBrides are a clan. Sly, Maggie, and I are more of a three-sister clan-ette.

"Not really," I say. "Tomorrow, Nick and Levi are joining the task force in Missoula that's focused on finding the traffickers. Hopefully, they will have some new information that will bring Sierra home."

When I consider what Sierra is facing, my throat tightens.

She must be terrified. I whisper the same prayer I've repeated many times since she called Nick three nights ago. "Please, God, keep Sierra safe and bring her home soon."

I glance at Grace and see tears trickling through the freckles that dust her cheeks.

"Hey." I touch her arm. "God's got this. We have to trust Him."

Grace swipes at the tears and nods.

"Since we're in Dillon, let's stop and see Verity," I suggest, hoping to lighten our moods.

"I'd like that." Grace says.

I turn the car toward downtown Dillon to Verity's shop. Last month, Grace took me to the specialty shop to find accessories for our homecoming outfits. It surprised me to discover that Verity and my mom had been friends.

Since my parents' murder a year ago, I treasure every memory of them. When Verity shared some conversations they'd had, I felt like Mom was with us, just for a few minutes.

THE BELL over Verity's door announces our arrival, and I stop to inhale the unique scent of the store. The fragrant tang of apple cider, mixed with the spicy aroma of freshly baked snickerdoodle cookies, smells delicious.

Verity stands behind the antique table that serves as a sales counter. At the tinkling of the bell, she looks up and gives us a dazzling smile. She nods toward a table holding the treats even as she speaks with two women standing at the counter.

"Yes, the ghost town of Bannack is a fascinating place, especially if you like history. I'm sorry that it's closed for the season. Maybe you can visit in the spring."

The women have a variety of items laid out on the table, but I'm not clear if they are buying or selling. I nudge Grace, and we head over to the cookie table to wait until Verity is free.

"Oh man," Grace mumbles around a mouthful of cookie. "These are amazing."

I lift the lid of the small slow cooker and ladle hot apple cider into two paper cups, then hand one to Grace. She takes a sip, and her eyes widen.

"Delicious and ... spicy?" She peers into the cup. "What do you think she added to the cider?"

I taste it and grin. "Red Hots. That's how Mamma used to make cider too."

I sip again, close my eyes, and for a moment, I hear Mamma and Daddy in our kitchen discussing how many Red Hots to put in the cider.

"Brian," Mamma said, "The recipe calls for one cup of Red Hots, not one entire bag."

"If some is good, more is better." Daddy reached around her and tried to pour more of the spicy candy into the large pot on the stove.

I smile, remembering how Mamma waved her wooden spoon at him, shooing him away. Daddy retreated, only to swoop back, kiss Mamma on the cheek, and drop a handful of candy into the pot.

The sound of raised voices interrupts my tender memory.

"Uh-oh," Grace whispers. "Sounds like Verity is having some trouble."

"It's worth a lot more than that!" The duo at the counter have added additional items to the pile they're trying to sell to Verity. "See how it shines? It could be pure gold."

Grace and I approach as Verity pulls a large magnet from a drawer.

"Let's check," she says with a tight smile. She picks up the gold-colored ring, and it clings to the magnet.

"I'm sorry," Verity says, kind but firm. "Gold is not magnetic, so this piece is gold-plated. It's a pretty ring, and I'm certain I can resell it, but I'll only pay the price I quoted."

I study the items the women have displayed. Most are

costume jewelry, and I assume Verity won't buy them for resale in her store.

The older woman is wearing skinny jeans and a leopard print jacket. She has what Sly calls 'big hair,' and as I get closer, her heavy perfume takes my breath away. She scoops up the items and stuffs them into a backpack with more force than necessary.

"Wait." The younger woman says. "Here's something." She reaches into the pocket of her baggy jeans and pulls out a necklace and reverently lays it down.

We press closer. Attached to a delicate gold chain is a single, vertical gold bar. A topaz stone glitters near the bottom of the bar, with the initial *S* engraved in the middle.

"That is lovely," Verity says. "But are you sure you want to sell such a personal piece?"

Leopard Woman gasps, then turns it into a cough. "Honestly ... Susie," the woman stammers. "Put that away. There's no need for you to sell your favorite necklace." She plucks up the necklace and stuffs it into her backpack with the other jewelry. Then she grabs Susie by the arm and sweeps her toward the exit.

"Susie," I call out, but both women keep moving. "Susie!"

Leopard Woman stops and nudges Susie, who slowly turns.

"Happy birthday," I say with what I hope appears to be a genuine smile.

Her forehead scrunches in confusion. "What?"

"Well, happy birthday month," I explain.

Susie shakes her head, "My birthday is in July."

Leopard Woman drags her through the door and onto the sidewalk. I follow them, ignoring the still tinkling bell. They hustle down the sidewalk, jump into a dirty brown SUV, and race off.

I hurry back into the shop, repeating a series of letters and numbers. Verity and Grace stare at me.

"Verity, do you have a pen and paper?" I ask breathlessly.

Without a word, Verity produces them, and I write the

identification I memorized from the license plate. Finally, I take a deep breath. "I need to call Nick."

"Jess, what's going on?" Verity asks. "Did you know those women?"

"No. But if that girl's name is Susie, I'm Taylor Swift. She said her birthday is in July, which has a ruby for the birthstone. The topaz stone is for November."

I pull out my phone and speed-dial Nick's number.

"I've seen that necklace before," I say. "It belongs to Sierra."

2

Monday
November 11
3:00 p.m.

Sierra

Sophie and I lie huddled on a soiled mattress, and I don't want to think about what made those stains. The bed is the only item in the narrow room. A dwindling stream of sunlight filters through the slats of the walls.

When Garlic Breath and the two women brought us here, they tied dirty rags over our eyes, so I have no idea where we are. I tried to pay attention as we rode in the SUV driven by the older woman, while Garlic Breath held a gun on us. When we arrived, I heard a car door slam. The younger woman must have followed in my Escort.

I'd managed to peek under the blindfold and caught a glimpse of a wooden structure that might have been called a cabin in its better days.

Sophie and I were thrust into this squalid room and heard the door lock behind us.

Now I watch Sophie, relieved that she can sleep. Sophie's had a rough life already, and in some ways, she's handled our captivity better than I have. I touch the dog tags dangling from the chain around my neck and lightly rub my thumb over the name engraved on them. Captain Jonathan Gallagher, USMC. At least the younger woman hadn't stolen them with the rest of my jewelry. They weren't considered valuable. Except by me.

I'm not sure exactly what time it is, but I suspect it's Monday evening. At first, I was afraid the kidnappers would leave us here with no food or water. But after several hours, the younger woman, whom I'd heard Garlic Breath call Rochelle, brought us some cheese and peanut butter crackers and two miniature bottles of water. About an hour later, the older woman, Daphne, hustled us to the outhouse and back to the cabin like she was being timed.

At some point on Saturday evening, Rochelle brought us a feast of Kodiak Krackers and apple juice. Sophie looked at the offering and scoffed, "What is this, kindergarten?" During the ensuing argument, I managed to swipe Rochelle's cell phone from her back pocket.

As soon as she left the room, I called my cousin Nick, a deputy sheriff, but before I could say much more than, "Help!" Rochelle stormed into the room and grabbed the phone from me. She also took my apple juice.

The past few days have been terrifying, but I'm more convinced than ever that Garlic Breath was incorrect. I wasn't in the wrong place. If I hadn't been in the park to meet Sophie, she would have disappeared—maybe forever. God placed me there to help her get home. I hope Nick can find us, but I don't plan to wait around to be rescued. We're going to find a way out.

3

Monday
November 11
5:00 p.m.

Jess

"Did you identify the owner of the SUV?" I'm barely through my front door before I pepper Nick with questions. "Do you think they have Sierra? Are you going to Dillon right now?"

Nick raises his hand to stop me. "Whoa, one question at a time." He's standing in the center of the living room, all official in his sheriff's deputy uniform.

"I ran the plates, and they came back to a 2017 Ford Escape belonging to a seventy-year-old grandmother living in a retirement home."

"So, they are kidnappers and car thieves?" I ask.

"Could be."

Sly distracts Nick when she enters the room carrying a plate of sandwiches. He grabs one that appears to be ham and Swiss and takes a healthy bite. "Thanks, this is the first chance I've had to eat."

Nick has barely stopped moving since he received Sierra's call. He and his dad drove over two hours to Missoula to meet with an FBI task force that is investigating human traffickers. They'd arrived back in Justice yesterday and were about to return to Missoula when I called Nick about the two women.

Now his investigation will focus on the area around Dillon and Justice, which I'm sure is a relief for Sly. My sister and Nick have only been a couple for a few weeks, and Sly is still learning how to adapt to the demands of Nick's job as deputy sheriff.

"Let's head back to Dillon, and I can help you locate the SUV," I offer, vibrating with excitement. "We could have Sierra home by tonight."

Nick takes a swig of the sweet tea Sly handed him. "It won't be necessary for you to come along. We have every law enforcement agency in the county looking for her. You gave an excellent description of the vehicle and the women. We can take it from here."

For the first time, I notice Deputy Levi Cooper, Nick's trainee, sitting in my dad's recliner. He has a ham sandwich and a fistful of chips. He chews, swallows, then smiles at me. "Good work, Jess."

I feel my cheeks heat a little at his praise.

Levi is not as tall as Nick or Cole, but his arms are all wiry muscle. When he first arrived in Justice, he was still wearing a short, military haircut, but now his blond hair has a little curl. His dark blue eyes are "almost navy," according to Grace.

During this description, I reminded Grace she already has a boyfriend, Kellen, who is much closer to our age.

"That doesn't mean I'm blind. He's easy to look at," Grace said.

Attractive or not, now I frown at Levi, who will take my place in the squad car. He doesn't seem disturbed, though, as he smiles. "Jess, you have good instincts. Have you considered law enforcement?"

"Don't encourage her," Nick says with a sigh. "Sheriff Herman is considering starting a new department to monitor Jess."

"Well, that's harsh." Grace wraps her arm around me and squeezes. "I think Jess has done a lot of good with her investigations. Robert Sinclair and Anthony Avery wouldn't be in jail if it wasn't for her."

"It's not the outcome Nick objects to, it's the method." Behind me, Cole's deep voice carries a hint of a smile. He must have entered the room when I was arguing with Nick.

I face him, and the stress of the past few hours drifts away. Cole has that effect on me.

"Jess, I appreciate your help." Nick's tone is sincere. "But we're already missing one member of the family. I don't want to add you to the list."

My heart skips a little at his words that show he considers us family. Before my parents were killed, they were friendly with Nick and Cole's parents. But in recent months, as relationships developed between Cole and me, and now Nick and Sly, we have become family. Sierra is their cousin and my friend. More family.

Nick and Levi finish their meal and take off for Dillon without me.

Sly whisks away the empty sandwich plate but returns with a refill. As Cole, Grace, and I eat, Sly fills us in on the search for Sierra.

"Nick and Levi interviewed Sierra's roommate again today. Gwen mentioned that Sierra's been concerned about one of the young girls in her mentoring class in Dillon. Her name is Sophie, and she lives with her mom, who struggles with drug addiction. Sierra was planning to spend some extra time with Sophie last weekend when she went to Dillon."

Sly settles into her favorite chair, a floral wingback my mother always used. Sly's dark hair makes her resemblance to

Mamma that much stronger. It's styled in a short, sleek bob that's casual and sophisticated. Not like my chestnut curls, whose style can be labeled "wild abandon."

"Wait, does that mean they don't think traffickers took Sierra?" Grace asks.

"They haven't ruled it out, but when Nick contacted her bank, they found she charged gas to her debit card on Friday afternoon in Deer Lodge. Since that's between Missoula and Dillon, it suggests she traveled in that direction."

"That's useful news," Cole says. "If traffickers took Sierra, it will be difficult to locate her, especially since they could be in Canada by this time."

"Right," Grace adds. "It's scary those two women we saw could have taken Sierra, but at least they're close by and should be easy to locate."

I stand and step to the window, feeling restless. I need to do something.

Cole comes to stand beside me. "We have to trust Nick and Levi. And God. He loves Sierra more than we do."

"I agree. But it's hard for me to stay back and do nothing. I want to hop in Sly's Honda and drive up and down the streets of Dillon, yelling Sierra's name."

"Well, I doubt they are yelling out the window," Cole says. "But Nick and Levi have lots of tools to help them locate her. And you gave them a great head start today. I'm proud of you."

When my tears leak, I am as surprised as Cole. Embarrassed, I duck my head, but he wraps me in his arms. "You don't hear that enough from me. I'm always frustrated when you take chances, but never doubt I am proud of you."

I nod, still not able to form words, and he chuckles. "Wow, if I knew it was this easy to make you speechless, I would have said it long ago."

Swiping at my eyes, I say, "I was worried you wouldn't want me involved in the search for Sierra. I'm glad you're okay with it."

"Well, that's not exactly what I said." Cole steps back, and his gray eyes are serious. "I understand and accept you'll always need to solve any mystery that shows up. It's even possible that's the way God created you. But He also made you smart, and part of being smart is recognizing when to be cautious."

"Don't worry, Cole. These last few months have more than fulfilled my desire for danger and excitement. I'll do everything I can to help find Sierra. But I plan to stay in the background and not take chances. Trust me, you have nothing to worry about."

4

Jess

"Maggie, let's move," I yell up the stairs at my thirteen-year-old sister. I catch a flash of dark hair as she rushes from the bathroom to her bedroom. Outside a horn beeps twice, and I hurry to the front door to wave at Grace, who is waiting not so patiently in her Civic. We've started taking turns driving to school, and Tuesday is her day. After school, I'll travel with Cole to my part-time job at Hadley's Ranch.

"I'm ready." I jump and turn to see Maggie grinning up at me.

"You're like a mini-ninja," I gripe as I open the door and follow her to the car. Maggie is a gymnast, and she moves with a smooth energy I envy.

Our day begins as I clamber into the passenger seat.

"Any news?" Grace glances at me, then back at the road. Like me, Grace is a newish driver, and she positions her hands at two

21

and ten, scrutinizing her side and rearview mirrors as she pulls from the driveway.

"Nothing. This morning during breakfast, Nick called Sly and said they spent the night searching for the SUV. No luck."

I glance out the window, observing kids heading to school. Some travel in groups, laughing and teasing. Others trudge alone, and I think of Sierra. She's alone, too. I feel the restlessness building. I wish I could skip school for the day and go to Dillon to help Nick and Levi search.

For a brief moment, I consider how to make that happen, then stop, imagining Nick's response when I appear in the middle of a school day, ready to join the search party. Nope. Hard pass.

Grace pulls the Civic up to the curb at Justice Junior High, and Maggie hops out with a quick, "Thanks, 'bye!" tossed over her shoulder. In the next instant, a sea of eighth graders sweeps her away.

"Were we ever that young?" Grace asks with an exaggerated sigh.

"Probably. I try to forget."

Grace parks the car at the far end of the high school lot, and we join the other latecomers who are racing to beat the bell. In two years, Grace and I will use the closer parking spots reserved for seniors. But for now, we run.

Grace disappears into the girls' locker room to get ready for her first-period PE class. My first class of the day is trig. Then the worst is out of the way.

As the day goes on, I struggle to keep my mind off Sierra. At lunch, I stop at my locker to check my phone for a message from Sly, but there's nothing.

When I hop into Cole's truck at three o'clock, I consider lobbying for a quick trip to Dillon before we go to work at Hadley's. But I assume the answer will be *no*. Instead, I ask, "Have you heard anything from Nick today?"

He points to his phone lying in the console's well. "You check."

I enter Cole's password to find three notifications. Touching the button, my heart pounds as I scan through the texts.

"Your mom needs you to pick up milk after work." I relay the message, then scroll down to Nick's name and read the text out loud.

"No sign of SUV or Sierra yet. Tell Mom that Levi and I will stop by for a bite before we leave. Later."

I sigh and return the phone to the console.

"They have the plates, too, Jess. If it's findable, Nick will find it." Cole swings the truck onto the gravel drive leading to Hadley's Ranch.

"After dinner, I'll ask Nick if we can help. We can knock on doors and ask if anyone has seen the car or Sierra. I feel it too, Jess. I want to do something."

Cole's jaw is tight, and I suspect he's as frustrated as I am. Although Sierra is his cousin, Cole has always treated her more like a sister. The thought of her being alone and in danger must be killing him.

I keep active cleaning stalls while Cole exercises Chieftain, Bob Hadley's prize stallion. Pushing the wheelbarrow toward the wide doorway, I stop to pat the small mare, Daisy.

Last month, Daisy and I had an adventure together as we searched for Joey, a lost five-year-old boy. During the search, we also found something we didn't want to—a deadly cougar. Daisy and I are friends for life.

I push away another unwelcome memory from that day— Amy Sinclair riding off with Cole to join the search. I'm confident Cole isn't interested in Amy, but that picture is a nettle that continues to irritate me.

Daisy whinnies and nudges my hand with her nose, encouraging more petting. I wish I had a treat to give her. "Carrots next time," I promise.

Daisy nickers, and I turn to see Cole astride Chieftain.

"Saddle up," Cole says. "The horses can use the exercise, and we need to clear our minds."

In minutes, we're racing across the field, and with each step, more stress drains away.

Cole leads us to a favorite spot that offers an expansive view of the Pioneer Mountains. Snow covers the jagged peaks. From this distance, peace settles over them, but a closer look would reveal the residents. Bears, wolves, and, yes, cougars. I shiver at the memory of the cougar, Outlaw, that terrorized our town.

"Cold?" Cole loops the horses' reins to a tree branch and raises his arms to lift me from the saddle. I can dismount on my own, of course, but I never pass up an opportunity to be in Cole's arms.

My feet touch the ground, but instead of letting me go, he pulls me closer. At first, the denim of his jacket is rough on my skin, but he opens it to offer the soft sherpa lining and I snuggle against his chest.

We stand like that for long minutes, not speaking. The warmth I feel goes all the way to my heart, and I smile in contentment.

Chieftain snorts and paws the ground restlessly.

"I think that's our cue." Cole grins, and I step back to look up, waiting for his kiss. It's tender and much too brief.

"Back to reality," I say, turning toward Daisy.

I'm surprised when Cole tugs me to him for another hug. "Jess, this *is* our reality." Tears tighten my throat. I want so much for that to be true. Forever.

It's already dark when we're back on the road to Justice. Cole drops me off at my house with the promise to call after he talks to Nick.

As I walk into the kitchen, I smell the unmistakable scent of Sly's meatloaf. She uses a recipe our mamma got from her mother, but Sly adds a few extras, including hot sauce. It's delicious.

Dinner is quiet as we think about Sierra. Through the years

we sat at this table with her, decorating cookies, playing Uno, and sharing secrets.

Sierra was the first to ask me about my feelings for Cole.

"Is there something you want to tell me?" Sierra's brown eyes sparkled with teasing as we dusted red and blue sprinkles over white, frosting-covered cookies. The Justice Fourth of July town picnic was the next day, and Sly had been cooking and baking all week. Sierra and I were the only ones in the house, and she waited for my answer.

"Yes. The red sprinkles belong on the bells, and the blue sprinkles on the stars." I tried to distract her, but she could be relentless. She wasn't asking about sprinkles.

"No, I mean, is there something going on between you and Cole?" She stopped sprinkling and touched my hand to stop me too. "There's a new ... electricity, I guess, between the two of you. Or is it my imagination?"

I shook my head, staring down at the cookies. "I hope that's true," I whispered. "At least, I'm feeling it. I'm not sure about Cole."

Sierra squeezed my hand and picked up a decorated cookie. "You have nothing to worry about. I'm pretty sure he's feeling it too." She broke the cookie and offered me half. "Here, let's celebrate." She gasped as we heard Sly coming through the back door and she tried to cram the cookie in her mouth.

"What's going on here?" Sly asked, coming to stand by the table.

"Nothing." Sierra giggled as she looked up at Sly, her eyes wide with innocence. Too bad frosting and red sprinkles covered her mouth.

Sudden tears sting my eyes at the memory, and I stand to carry my plate to the counter. Sly follows and, although I'm sure she saw the tears, she doesn't mention them. Instead, she says, "I'll make up some meatloaf sandwiches for you to take to the guys when you leave for Dillon."

Surprised, I gape at her. "I'm going to Dillon?"

"Yes. Nick texted earlier and said they could use you and Cole to knock on doors, if you're willing."

"Of course." I reach for my phone. "I'll ask if Grace wants to go along."

"That's fine." Sly pulls out bread for the sandwiches. "Tell Cole he can drive my car if you three don't want to be crowded into the cab of his truck."

I give her a quick hug and hurry upstairs to grab an extra jacket, wool cap, and gloves.

Finally, I have a job to do.

But at eleven that night we return to Justice exhausted and discouraged. No one has seen Sierra. Nick and Levi stay in Dillon, planning to grab some much-needed sleep at the sheriff's office. They'll start the search again in the morning. For now, all we can do is pray Sierra is safe.

5

Tuesday
November 12
1:00 p.m.

Sierra

"Sophie?" I touch her arm. "I think they're discussing what to do with us."

She joins me near the door, where I sit, my long legs folded under me on the hard plank floor. As we press our ears against the rough boards, our captors' voices carry, and we scoot closer to catch every word.

"This plan isn't working out." Garlic Breath sounds agitated, and the stomping of his boots echoes across the floor of the cabin's main room. "We were 'sposed to get the drugs from Travis by now so we could meet the cartel. Now we got two whiny girls we gotta keep fed and watered."

"They're not houseplants, Clive." Daphne's voice sounds a little amused.

Sophie and I glance at each other with raised eyebrows and mouth the name, *Clive*. That's not the name I would have guessed for Garlic Breath. He reminds me more of a Joe-Bob or Bubba. Clive? Not so much.

"Well, I think they're kind of sweet," Rochelle says, and I can picture Garlic Breath—um, Clive—glowering at her. "What?" she continues. "They're nice. See the necklace the older one gave me?"

I clench my jaw to keep from shouting through the door that my necklace was not a gift. Mom gave it to me last year for my nineteenth birthday. I'll turn twenty on Thanksgiving Day. Tears sting my eyes. Will I even be able to celebrate with my family?

I run my fingers across the worn dog tags still hanging around my neck. When Rochelle saw those, she dismissed them as junk, in favor of my birthstone necklace. I wanted to shout at her that the dog tags weren't worthless. My dad had given everything for them.

Daphne sounds impatient. "Rochelle, that girl didn't give you the necklace. You stole it from her. Didn't you try to pawn it yesterday?"

"Well, she didn't fight for it, did she?" Rochelle is determined to stick to her story.

"Could be that was 'cause I was holding a gun on her," Clive points out.

"*Hmm.*" She doesn't seem convinced, and for a second, I feel sorry for her. Has anyone ever given her a gift?

"Back to the point," Clive snaps. "Travis disappeared with the cartel's drugs, and if he doesn't return them by Saturday, we're all dead. Including those two sweet girls," he finishes with a sneer.

"I've been thinking," Daphne says.

"Uh oh,"

Rochelle stops mid-giggle at Clive's terse, "Shut up!"

Daphne continues, "If we don't have the drugs, what if we give the cartel money instead? That's what the drugs are for, right? To make them some money."

"You're so smart," Rochelle says, admiration in her voice.

"Now why didn't I think of that?" Clive's words drip with

sarcasm. "I'll go down to the basement and fire up my handy-dandy money machine and print out what we need. I'll even print out more than we need for the cartel, and you girls can have some mall money. How does that sound?"

To me, it sounds like Clive is getting angrier by the second, but Daphne ignores him.

"I'm just saying we need a back-up plan." Daphne's tone is impatient. "If Travis doesn't show with the drugs, maybe we can make a withdrawal from the Justice Savings and Loan on Saturday morning." I picture her making air quotes around the word *withdrawal*.

"Yay." Rochelle claps her hands in excitement. "I always wanted to rob a bank!"

"What are we going to do?" Sophie gnaws around the edge of her stale granola bar, weighing her hunger against the genuine possibility of breaking a tooth.

I tip up my mini water bottle and drain the last drop. Our captors must be stingy with the water bottles because they don't like the chore of escorting us to the outhouse. They take us out twice a day, whether we need it or not. Having a pistol waving between the two of us always puts me in an outhouse frame of mind.

"We're going to escape."

Sophie gives me a questioning squint that reminds me of a famous line from an old television show. *What you talkin' about, Willis?* I've never heard of Willis, but apparently, he says a lot of crazy stuff.

"How?" My words must distract Sophie, since she takes a big bite of her granola bar, giving no thought to the consequences. I hear a *crack,* and Sophie's eyes widen as she pulls the bar away from her mouth.

"Can't look," she mumbles, keeping her mouth closed. I lean closer, relieved there is no tooth attached.

"Open up."

Sophie opens her mouth to show me all her pearly white teeth are intact.

"You're good," I say.

She wraps the bar and puts it in her jeans pocket. "I'll try again later."

Abruptly overwhelmed by our situation, I flop back onto the rickety cot. When I left Missoula on Friday afternoon, I'd worn my softest jeans and my maroon Grizzlies sweatshirt. Actually, since signing with the Grizzlies volleyball team, most of my clothes are maroon. But over the past few days, my jeans have become caked with dirt and scratchy on my skin.

I shift uncomfortably on the cot, which lurches beneath me, and the next thing I know, I'm flying to crash on the hard floor. A metal screw rolls across the floor as the bed frame separates and collapses.

Sophie and I hold our breath and listen for noise from the other room. Silence. I relax and turn my attention to the destroyed bed. Clive will not approve.

I glance at Sophie. I can't identify her expression— somewhere between horror and ... hope. That's new.

"I think I have an idea." Sophie scrambles off the tilted bed and stands. She pulls up the cuff of her jeans to display yellow socks peeking out from her sneakers. She grins, the first I've seen since our abduction, and slides her hand inside the sock and pulls out a small silver spoon.

My first thought is *Ew,* but I ask, "Soph, why do you have a spoon hidden in your sock?" It sounds like a reasonable question.

Sophie shrugs then hurries over to the broken side of the bed. "When Daphne came to pick up our oatmeal dishes this morning, I sat on it. I figured if she noticed it missing, I could act like it was an accident. But she didn't notice, so I kept it."

She peers up at me through the curtain of light brown hair

hanging limply around her face. The pink streaks she recently applied to the strands are already fading, and for some reason that makes me unreasonably sad. She gives me a quizzical look when she notices my expression.

"This might work better than digging our way out." She waves the spoon in the air.

I shake off the sadness, kneel next to her, and watch as she tries to slide the flat end of the spoon into the screw that holds the bed together.

"If we can loosen this screw, we can pull this metal bar free, and we'll have a weapon."

At the word *weapon*, my stomach lurches and I move back a little. I'm not sure I could use the bar to hurt someone, but I don't share that with Sophie. Besides, they have guns, and I doubt Clive, at least, is afraid to use his. We may not have a choice.

The bedframe squeaks a bit, and Sophie stops her task as we both hold our breath, listening. A nest of mice rustles under the wooden floor in the quiet room.

I release my breath and tiptoe to the door, pressing my ear against the rough boards. Then I squint through the space between the slats. Rochelle is pacing in front of the rickety table, talking on her burner phone. I remember holding that same phone in my hands a few days earlier, when I called Nick to tell him about the kidnapping. He must be looking for us, but it feels like our time is running out. We have to escape. Now.

"No, I don't know where Clive went," Rochelle says into the phone. "He took off about five minutes after you left for the grocery store." She listens for a minute then says, "Pick me up another phone, would you? This one is almost dead."

My heart flips. Clive and Daphne are both gone, leaving us alone with Rochelle. If we want to escape, this is the moment.

6

Tuesday
November 12
3:00 p.m.

Sierra

S canning the small room, I search for anything I can use to
contain Rochelle. I hurry to the bed and grab the dingy
blanket, softly whispering to Sophie, "Rochelle's alone. It's time
to go."

Sophie nods and resumes her project of trying to dismantle
the bed frame. I slip over to the door and peek through it again.
The metal rod hits the wall with a clang, alerting Rochelle, and
she swings her head around to face our room. She frowns at her
phone, holds it to her ear, then slams it down on the table.
"Junk," she mutters.

At that moment, the metal frame clatters to the floor.
Rochelle hurries to our door and I turn to watch Sophie
struggling to lift the metal rod.

"Leave it," I say as I feel Rochelle pushing against the door to
lift the heavy wooden beam that serves as the lock. I wave

Sophie over and she joins me, giving a regretful glance back at the piece of metal she'd worked so hard to free.

I hand Sophie one edge of the blanket, whispering. "We'll throw it over her head and push her into the room."

Sophie nods like this is the most brilliant plan she's ever heard. I give our chances fifty-fifty.

We stand behind the door as Rochelle swings it wide. She stops without entering the room, surprised it's empty. Then she stalks inside and barks, "Hey, you two. Where'd you go?"

As she approaches the middle of the room, we rush her, lifting the blanket high, covering her head, and securing her arms at her sides. I give her a hearty shove and wince as she flies across the room to land on the broken bed.

As she's trying to fight her way out of the blanket, she cries, "Clive is gonna kill me!" I hesitate for a second, but Sophie grabs my hand and pulls hard. We fly through the doorway and slam the heavy door, then lift the wooden beam to lock Rochelle inside.

Sophie runs to the table and grabs the phone and I hate how her expression of hope turns to desperation when I say, "It's dead."

Sophie slips it into her jeans pocket, and we run out of the cabin into the still-bright sunshine. I put my hand over my eyes. They locked us in that room for four days, and we have to adjust to the light.

We stop in the grass in front of the cabin and turn in circles, trying to determine the best direction to run. There's a worn trail leading to the cabin, but it can't be called a road. We might meet Clive or Daphne if we go that way.

I wish I'd paid more attention in Pioneer Girls when we had the lesson on wilderness camping. Just knowing north, south, east, and west might be helpful.

Sophie touches my arm and points to our left. "Dillon is south." I glance around one more time, then I follow her to freedom.

7

Tuesday
November 12
11:30 p.m.

Sierra

I wake up as I fall off the rock bench.

Beside me, Sophie is snoring, and I'm relieved she can sleep. At least when she's asleep, she's not scared, cold, or hungry. Then I realize what woke me. Sophie will feel that same urge soon too.

Sophie's voice whispers in the darkness. "Sierra? I have to go to the bathroom."

Ugh. Her urgency powers my own, and I accept that our time in the relative safety of the cave is done.

After a few attempts I find her hand. "Okay, Soph, let's go find the bathroom."

We crawl through the darkness of the cave and emerge into the forest. At least there's a moon tonight. Pointing to some bushes growing to the right of the cave entrance I say, "I'll keep an eye out—you can go first."

Although I expect some complaints, Sophie hurries to the bushes without a word. I glance around, trying to remember what the landscape was like when we entered the cave. Mostly, there are trees. And more trees.

Sophie returns, and I make my way to the bushes. When we join up again, we take a minute to discuss strategy. Run. Sounds like a good plan, but which direction?

We climb a hill away from the cave to find a better view. Once we're there, the wind flares, and I start to shiver. Glancing around, I freeze. A small light bobs through the forest.

Garlic Breath.

I turn to warn Sophie as she points in the opposite direction and says, "There!"

In the distance, the twinkling lights of Dillon, Montana are visible. Safety.

Without a word, I shift Sophie toward the approaching flashlight, and she gasps. It occurs to me it could be a searcher, but no one is shouting our names. It has to be Clive. The decision is simple.

"Run." Although I whisper the word, in my mind it's like a shout. I grab Sophie's hand and race toward the lights of Dillon. Tree branches brush my arms and scratch my face. I imagine they are the hands of the kidnapper and pull Sophie closer to me. I don't want to become separated from her. If I thought it was hard to run in the forest during the daylight, it's impossible in the dark.

After a moment of crashing through the trees, it hits me, we are making enough noise to attract our pursuer's attention. I slow down, whispering, "We need to be as quiet as possible."

Sophie's whisper carries a hint of exasperation. "I'm not the one who took off like a herd of elephants."

"Right." I slow my pace even more and glance over my shoulder. The flashlight beam is nowhere in sight, but the glowing lights of Dillon spur my hope. We move on.

"Ouch!" Sophie's startled cry makes my heart skip a beat. What if Clive heard?

Sophie is kneeling on the ground, a grimace of pain visible in the moonlight. "I think I stepped in a rabbit hole." She gingerly touches her ankle and stifles another groan.

I kneel beside her and touch the swelling ankle. "Not broken, but it could be sprained." I bite my lip, trying to think of what to do. Earlier, I was sure we'd make it off this mountain and into the safety those distant lights represent. But they're so far away, they may as well be the stars.

"I can walk." Sophie grunts, stands, and takes a hobbling step. I catch her before she falls and wrap my arm around her waist.

"Here, put your arm over my shoulder," I tell her. On the plus side, our combined body heat is a welcome relief from the falling temperature. We move on, trying to stay in the shadows and out of the moonlight. We can do this. But hope evaporates when a voice calls from the trees behind us.

"C'mon, Sierra, I only want Sophie. Leave her with me and you can go on home," Clive lies. He'll never let me go, even if I give him Sophie, and that will never happen.

"I won't hurt her. She's a little insurance to make sure her Uncle Travis returns the drugs he stole from us. Soon as he does, Sophie is free." Clive's voice sounds closer now.

"Maybe I should go with him?" Sophie's voice shakes with her brave and unacceptable offer.

"Sophie, he's lying. He won't let you go, even if your uncle brings back the drugs. Clive will kill you or possibly send you off with traffickers. Whatever happens, he won't let you go."

"This isn't your problem." The harshness of her words sting. She can't mean them. But Sophie said those words many times when we first met. It had taken a few meetings for me to understand she's used to being on her own.

My heart broke for her as she navigated her unstable living

situation. Sophie may be young, but she has more courage than many adults. I won't let her go back with Clive.

"I can't walk all the way down the mountain. We both get that. But if I go with him, he will let you go and you can send help." Determination mixed with fear trembles in her voice.

"Absolutely not!" I try to give my words that 'don't mess with me' tone, but it's hard to do with chattering teeth. "Stay here."

I move up a small incline, hoping for a better view. Chancing a glance, my heart sinks when I spot the bobbing flashlight beam headed right for Sophie.

"Sophie!" My harsh whisper of warning is carried away by the howling wind.

Scrambling down the hill I stop behind a large pine tree. I peek around, where is she?

Bark flies and debris from the tree hits my cheek.

The shock of a literal slap in the face gives me pause. I finally register the gunshot echoes in the night's stillness. I wait for another shot, but the forest is quiet and I crawl toward the last place I saw Sophie.

She's gone.

8

Jess

"How do I let you talk me into these things?" Grace offers me a strawberry Pop-Tart, taking the sting from her words.

"Honestly, Grace, I meant what I said. I can go by myself and be back in time to pick you up for school. There's no reason for you to take a chance of getting in trouble."

"Nope, I'm in," Grace assures me. "My only condition is I'm able to gripe whenever I want."

"Sold." I grin at my best friend. "And you have Pop-Tart on your lip."

Grace pulls down the visor to examine herself in the mirror, daintily removing the crumb. While she's at it, she fluffs her red-blond hair and takes a half-hearted swipe at the freckles dotting her nose. I don't get why she bothers. They never come off.

"You have a plan?" Grace mumbles around the Pop-Tart.

39

"We should take some of the back roads to see if we can spot anything suspicious. Nick and Levi have the majority of the town covered."

"Good idea," Grace says. "Plus, we can avoid being spotted by Nick."

Ten minutes later, we are slowly driving the back roads at the south end of Dillon.

It was dark when we left Justice, but now the sun is peeking through the canopy of trees lining the roadside. I'm thankful there's not much traffic, so I can drive slowly. We scan the forest on both sides, hoping to glimpse something.

"What if we run into those women again? You won't try to talk to them, will you? They could be dangerous." Concern edges Grace's question.

"No, I've already thought about that. If we see them, I'll call Nick and give him our location. If they try to leave, I'll follow, but not too close. I don't want a confrontation. I just want to find Sierra."

We're quiet for a few minutes, focusing on the trees.

"Um, Jess? Did you see that?" Grace points toward an opening in the trees on the right.

I tap the brakes and slow, then glance in the rear-view mirror. We have the entire road to ourselves, so I carefully back up to the point Grace indicates. A flash of maroon catches my eye and I say, "Roll down your window and yell."

Grace powers down the window, leans out as far as she dares, and hollers, "Sierra! Sierra, are you out there?"

My heart sinks when there is no sound. Then unexpectedly, Sierra is standing in the ditch, waving her arms.

"Here." she yells. "Please help me!"

I pull the Honda over and put on the emergency flashers. Grace and I tumble out of the car and race to where Sierra is climbing out of the ditch. She gapes at us as if she thinks she's hallucinating, then with a cry she hurries to wrap her arms around us.

"I should have guessed you two would find me." She's half laughing and half sobbing.

Grace and I are stunned, and for a moment we revel in the knowledge Sierra is with us, safe and sound.

"Climb in." I motion toward the Honda. "I'll call Nick and tell him they can stop searching. We've found you."

Sierra grabs my arm and pulls me to a stop. "No, they can't stop searching. The kidnappers still have Sophie."

WE'RE in a conference room at the Justice Sheriff's Department, sipping hot coffee and trying to eat bacon and egg biscuits. Deputy Levi Cooper is beside Sierra, taking notes as she describes the kidnappers and the cabin where she and Sophie were kept.

Nick is talking to Dillon's chief of police, coordinating the call for new searchers for Sophie. He finishes the conversation and joins Grace and me at the other end of the table, where we're nibbling on our own breakfast sandwiches.

"Does Sly know you stole her car?" He takes a sip of his coffee and studies me.

I choke a little at the word stole. "I didn't steal her car! This is my day to drive to school. Grace and I left a little early today. That's all."

"Yeah, by two hours," Grace mumbles around her hash browns.

"Let's try again. Does Sly know where you are?" Nick's gaze never wavers. He's stubborn like that.

"Yes, I texted her as soon as we got to the station. She wasn't exactly crazy about the fact we left town without telling anyone, but I think we made up for it by finding Sierra." I give him a bright smile that doesn't appear to impress him.

"You could have found a lot more than Sierra," Nick warns. "From what she told us, the kidnappers are armed and dangerous. What would you and Grace have done if you ran into them first and they shot at you?"

I open my mouth to explain my plan to drive away and go for help, but I hadn't factored in the possibility they might have guns. I close my mouth without speaking.

"Exactly." Nick nods and is about to continue the lecture, but Deputy Levi interrupts. Thank goodness.

"Hey, Nick, we may have a hit on the kidnapper based on Sierra's description. His name is Clive Kemp. He's a midlevel drug dealer from Missoula. Sierra said Kemp wanted some drugs that Sophie's Uncle Travis stole from the cartel. Kemp was planning to use Sophie as leverage to make Travis return the drugs. Unfortunately, Sierra got caught up in the plan."

Levi folds his arms across his broad chest, and I feel he'd like the chance to have a *chat* with Kemp. And Travis, too.

"I don't consider it bad luck." Sierra's voice is quiet but firm. "If I hadn't been there, Sophie would have been alone. At least now you know who has her and why. I only wish she hadn't gone with him when he found us on the mountain."

"You think she went voluntarily?" Nick asks. "Why would she do that?"

"She sprained her ankle and was afraid she was slowing me down. Clive was yelling at us and said he just wanted Sophie and that he'd let her go as soon as Travis returned the drugs. She knew he was lying, but she went with him to protect me." Sierra's lip quivers with the words.

"Brave girl," Levi observes. "Kind of stupid, but brave."

Sierra glares at him but says nothing. Her eyes tell the story, though. She is not a fan of Deputy Levi Cooper. At all.

"Sierra, where did you find the phone you used to call Nick?" This question has been on my mind for the past hour.

"When they first took us, Clive smashed our phones," Sierra explains. "But when the younger girl, Rochelle, brought us our dinner, such as it was, I noticed a phone in her jacket pocket. I accidentally on purpose stumbled into her, and she dropped the tray of food. While she was distracted, I grabbed her phone and slid it under the bed."

Deputy Cooper's eyebrows lift, and I think he's a little impressed by Sierra's courage.

"Wait." I hold up my hand to stop her. "The younger woman's name is Rochelle, and not Susie?"

A frown creases Sierra's forehead. "Who is Susie?"

"Never mind, they must have used fake names at Verity's. I *knew* her name wasn't Susie." I motion for Sierra to continue.

"As soon as she left, I dialed the McBride home number, explaining to Nick what was happening. But Rochelle missed her phone right away, so she came back and took it."

"I'm surprised they didn't move you immediately after they knew you'd made a call," Nick says. "It was an untraceable burner, but they couldn't be sure how much you told me."

"I don't think Rochelle told the other two what happened. She was probably scared she'd be in trouble for losing the phone in the first place." Sierra sighs. "That call didn't help at all."

"Not true," Nick says. "The call told us you were alive. That's *not* nothing." In a rare show of emotion, Nick hugs Sierra and she leans into his embrace. He clears his throat and continues, "We have some good info now, so we'll start a background check on Kemp's known associates. Maybe they can give us a clue to the cabin's location where they kept you girls."

He turns to Levi. "Will you drive Sierra back to my house? Aunt Connie is on her way and will meet you there."

"Wait." I step into the group. "Sierra, where is your car? You drove it down from Missoula, right?"

"Yes, but Clive took my keys and later gave them to Daphne."

"Leopard Woman," I say.

Sierra's eyes widen. "Perfect name for her. Anyway, my car was still at the cabin when Sophie and I escaped."

"That should make it easier to spot the right cabin. Was there a garage?" Nick asks.

"I didn't notice any other buildings. Just the falling down cabin." Sierra shivers.

Earlier the excitement of being found had buoyed Sierra, but now it's obvious she's exhausted and overwhelmed from her ordeal. I'm sure Sophie is never far from her mind.

Nick notices Sierra's slump, and he nods to his deputy. "Take her home, Levi." Nick breaks protocol and offers his cousin another quick hug. "I'm glad you're safe."

Sierra wraps her arms around Nick and squeezes. "Me too," she says, and her voice cracks a little.

Then she turns and follows Levi out the door.

9

Wednesday
November 13
10:00 a.m.

Sierra

I'm not being fair, but there's something about Deputy Levi Cooper that annoys me. A lot. I mean, sure, he's attractive if you like hulking, blue-eyed, blond men. He's not as tall as my cousins, but he makes up for it in the width of his shoulders.

Even in his uniform, I can tell he is well muscled. His wheat-blond hair is close-cropped, but it's curling a little on the top and sides. I'm sure he will put an end to that soon, though. I don't have any proof, but I feel he's recently left the military. Maybe that's why he comes across as so serious.

"Seen all you need to?" His voice startles me, and then his words sink in. He caught me studying him. Well, fine.

I try to cover my embarrassment with a shrug. "Probably," I say, then cringe. Probably? What does that mean? I shrug again like I mean it and turn to watch the countryside fly past the window of the sheriff's department's SUV. I think of the quiz that asks if you've ever ridden in a squad car.

Check.

It's quiet several minutes, and I feel Deputy Levi Cooper would be content to make the rest of the trip in silence. Too bad.

In the past three days, I've been kidnapped, starved, frozen, threatened with a gun, and terrorized. The relief of safety is waning, and now every emotion is surfacing, including the not-so-pretty ones. Anger, grief, fear. And despite the egg biscuit, hunger.

"I'd like to stop at the Dairy Barn on the way to my aunt's house." I try to make it sound like a request, but it comes out as a demand. That's not me at all, but right now I don't feel like me. I feel like if I soften at all, I'll melt into a puddle of tears. Fear for Sophie nags at me, disorienting my senses.

It's not the deputy's fault I'm an emotional mess. As I turn to apologize for my tone, Deputy Cooper smashes my good intentions with one word.

"No."

"No?" I hate the high pitch of my voice, but I continue. "What do you mean, 'No'? Let me remind you, I'm the victim here, not the perp."

His lips give a tiny twitch at my use of the word *perp*. I ignore that and continue my tirade. "I have rights, you know."

"Yep. Including the right to remain silent." His lips twitch again, and I eye him suspiciously.

"Is that a joke?" If I were in a better mood, I'd appreciate his attempt at humor. Sadly for Deputy Cooper, my mood is plummeting as fast as my blood sugar.

"Well, since the point of a joke is to elicit at least a smile, I guess it's not." He signals a right turn and takes the road to the McBride home.

A moment later we pass the Dairy Barn and I open my

mouth to say, "Stop," but then I spot the dreaded *Closed for the Season* sign.

"Oh," I say, defeated.

"You missed it by a week." I almost detect sympathy in Levi's voice. "But if it helps any, I heard Nick talking to your aunt on the phone. She was telling him about all the food she and Sly have been making. Hold on for two more minutes, and I'm sure Mrs. McBride will have a feast waiting for you."

"Thank you." I glance away as tears sting my eyes.

"You're welcome."

Suddenly, I need to make this right. "I'm sorry about being such a ... a ..."

"Brat?" he offers with a grin, and I nod.

"Yes, that."

His blue gaze turns serious. "Sierra, I understand trauma. Don't worry about it. Give yourself time to process what happened to you and your friend. And trust that Nick and I will do everything we can to find Sophie and lock up Kemp for good."

As we pull into the driveway, Uncle Malcolm throws open the front door. A moment later, I'm wrapped in my uncle's strong arms. Since Dad was killed in Afghanistan when I was eight, Uncle Mal has been like a father to me.

Aunt Mary places a gentle hand on my shoulder. "Goodness, Mal, let the girl breathe."

Uncle Malcolm barks a laugh and squeezes me one more time before stepping back. He turns to Levi. "Deputy Cooper, thank you for bringing her back to us."

The deputy shakes his head and holds up his hands. "I'd like to take the credit, but your niece found her own way to safety. With a little help from Jess and Grace."

"Girl power," Aunt Mary whispers in my ear, and I grin.

"Yes, Nick told us how that happened," Uncle Malcolm says. "I'm not sure how I feel about the girls taking off on their own, but the result was excellent, so I'll keep my thoughts to myself." He opens the front door and ushers us into the house and straight to the kitchen.

I breathe in the aroma of sweet rolls and coffee, and I'm reminded of my hunger. Aunt Mary hurries to set the rolls and coffee carafe on the sturdy kitchen table.

"Is my mom here?" I gaze around the cheerful room, suddenly longing for my mother.

"She's on her way," Aunt Mary assures me. "She's been in Missoula, searching for you. Nick thought it would be a good idea for her to stay there."

"She thought I ran away?" It had never occurred to me, but now I'm eager to see Mom. I can't imagine what she's been thinking and feeling over these past few days. I catch a glance between Aunt Mary and Uncle Malcolm. "What?"

"Connie said you haven't been responding to her calls or texts recently," Uncle Malcom explains. "She thought you might be avoiding her. She even called campus police to find you. Their report was that you weren't happy to be found. We were concerned you were spending time with people who might pull you away." He watches me with what I think of as his lawyer face, and I feel like I'm on the witness stand.

I nibble my lower lip. How should I respond? The truth is, I have been avoiding my mom lately, but not because I was doing anything wrong. I just need some independence. I feel my cheeks warm as guilt washes over me. I guess I was so focused on how I was feeling that I didn't consider Mom's needs.

"The night the campus police found me, I was having pizza with friends. It embarrassed me that Mom had called them to track me down, so I guess my response wasn't the best." I slump into a kitchen chair, exhausted. "Hurting Mom was never my plan, but I need some space. I need her to respect my decisions. At first, I started hanging out with some people who weren't as focused on school as they should be. But I figured that out fast and chose to stay away from them."

Uncle Mal nods. "I thought it might be something like that. You and your mom could talk about boundaries once things calm down."

Aunt Mary offers me a plate with a sweet roll, dripping with frosting. "In the meantime, relax and enjoy being safe."

I obey, eagerly reaching for the plate. I peek up to see Deputy Cooper watching me with that quirk on his mouth, but I don't care. Aunt Mary's sweet rolls are a legend in Justice, and I will not feel self-conscious. I lick the frosting from my fingers and take a bite. Heaven.

"Deputy, please take some rolls and coffee with you." Aunt Mary bustles around, filling a travel mug with coffee and placing four sweet rolls in a plastic container. "Two for you and two for Nicholas." She hands him the container and the coffee mug.

"Thank you, ma'am." Deputy Cooper looks like he would like to wolf down all four rolls himself, but since Nick is his boss, I figure he will share. He stares at me, and it appears he's choosing his words. Finally, he simply says, "Take care," and heads toward the door.

Aunt Mary joins me at the table and reaches for the coffee creamer. "Such a nice young man."

"I'm not sure I'd call him a nice young man." Uncle Malcolm settles next to me and scoops up a sweet roll.

"He's not nice?" The question pops out before I can stop it.

"Nice isn't the right word." My uncle considers this. "In fact, I'm not sure just one word can describe Deputy Cooper."

I watch him, waiting for more, but he smiles and takes a healthy bite of his roll.

"What about young?" My mouth keeps asking questions while my mind shouts, *be quiet.*

"*Hmm.*" Either Uncle Mal is calculating Deputy Cooper's age or he's really enjoying his sweet roll. "I think Nick mentioned the deputy is twenty-four. He recently finished a tour with the

Army Rangers and is using those skills in law enforcement. Nick tells us Levi is highly skilled and will make an excellent deputy."

I open my mouth to say, "Well, we've covered the nice and young part of the description. There is no question he's a man." Fortunately, my mind activates in time to prevent me, and I shove a bite of sweet roll into my mouth to stop the words.

Aunt Mary eyes me. "Sierra, I should have offered you something more substantial than pastries and coffee. You must be half-starved!" She hops up, no doubt to create a gourmet meal in five minutes.

I chew, swallow, then mumble, "No, Aunt Mary. This is more than enough." I'm exhausted and want to sleep. The adrenaline rush has dissipated.

"Is it possible to take a shower and a nap?" It takes all my energy to form the words.

"Of course, sweetheart." Aunt Mary leads me up the stairs to Piper's old room. They turned it into a guest room with its own bath after my cousin moved out. Piper has been married for over five years now, but I still remember how I loved visiting and having sleepovers here.

My aunt hurries to the closet and pulls out some gray sweatpants and a Justice High sweatshirt. "Your mom is bringing some clothes, but in the meantime, help yourself to anything that Piper left in this closet. They should fit you fairly well, although the pants may be a little short. I'm sure Piper will be happy to share."

Twenty minutes later, I sink into the bed, reveling in finally being clean again. Long blonde strands of hair escape from under the towel I have wrapped around my head. When I remove the towel, it will be a mass of unruly curls.

I'm curious what Deputy Cooper is doing, but I grit my teeth at the thought. This has to stop. I in turn remember a picture sitting on the mantel in our home. Dad, dressed in his Marine uniform. He's so handsome and strong. Indestructible. But he died in Afghanistan when I was eight years old. Still handsome and strong. But not indestructible.

Levi is no longer a soldier, but being a deputy isn't a safe job either. I'm proud of Nick, but how does Sly cope with knowing the man she loves could die on the job? Even after so many years, I remember my mom's sorrow as she grieved for my father. Now, I see the concern in Aunt Mary's and Sly's eyes when Nick walks out the door.

Pushing away thoughts of Deputy Levi Cooper, I vow that I'll never be *that* woman.

I reach for the towel, but the last of my energy is gone, and I sleep.

10

Wednesday
November13
6:00 p.m.

Jess

S leep deprivation is an ugly thing. I get bags under my eyes, and according to Maggie, I turn into a Crabby Patty. Add to that, I've just endured another lecture from Sly about my lack of communication skills. I want to point out that my skills are excellent. I just chose not to use them, but it seemed wiser to nod and appear penitent.

I'm sorry I worried Sly this morning. Yes, I found Sierra, and Sly gives me credit for that, but I admit it was the grace of God and not my great detecting ability. But I left town without telling anyone, taking Grace with me, and, apparently, that deserves a lecture. Fine. My bad.

I needed a nap after school, but I'm so far behind in my school assignments I made myself focus on homework. Now, I'm sleepy, crabby, and I have the kind of headache that only comes from doing twenty trigonometry problems.

Poor Cole. When he picks me up for our Bunch of Believers youth meeting, I'm in a terrible mood.

Climbing into the cab of Cole's truck, I slam the door, and put on my seatbelt, all without a word or a glance at him.

"Hi," he says tentatively.

"*Hmm*," I respond.

He pulls the truck out of the driveway and onto the road that leads out of town. BoB meets at Pastor Jarrod and Anna's farmhouse, about a ten-minute drive.

We're quiet for the first five. Then Cole tries again. "Good job finding Sierra."

I frown at him. "What's that supposed to mean?"

I startle a laugh from him.

"Good. Job. Finding. Sierra." He spreads the words out like he's examining each one for a hidden meaning. "Sounds straightforward to me." The smile in his voice irritates me.

"It was your tone." I return to my forward-facing pose.

"My. Tone." He spaces those words out, too, and I glare at him.

"Will you stop that?"

"Possibly. But only if you tell me what's wrong?"

"Nothing is wrong. Everything is just peachy." The tears stinging my eyes tell a different story.

"Was Sly mad you took her car to Dillon?"

"What do you think?" I'm being unreasonable, but I'm like an unstoppable runaway train.

"I think that, like me, Sly is unhappy with your whole 'ask for forgiveness but not permission' way of doing things."

"I wasn't aware I needed your permission," I snap.

Cole's jaw clenches slightly. "That's not what I said."

Replaying his words, I realize he's right. For a moment, I picture myself at a crossroads. I can either deliberately misunderstand and escalate this into a full-blown argument, or I can admit he's right. I sigh.

"Yes, I know," I concede, and the tension eases between us.

Cole pulls into the drive leading to the farmhouse and turns off the engine. I reach for the door handle, but he stops me with a quiet, "Jess."

I study him, really seeing him for the first time tonight. His warm gray eyes show telltale signs of exhaustion. We've all been under so much stress these past few days. Without thinking, I reach out to cup his face, running my thumb across his cheek. He turns his head and places a gentle kiss on my palm. Then he pulls me closer and I lean my head on his shoulder, feeling my tension ease.

We sit like that for long minutes, then Cole glances over my shoulder. "Don't look now, but we have an audience."

I tip my head down and feel the warmth of a blush. Great.

Cole grins and reaches for the door handle. "C'mon, let's go face the music."

When we walk into the family room, everyone is sitting in their places on sofas, chairs and, of course, on the floor. No one utters a word, but they all turn to watch us with big smiles. I can feel my cheeks pinken as I scurry to take my spot on the loveseat next to Grace.

"Okay." Pastor Jarrod stands in the middle of the room and asks the usual question. "How's everyone's week been so far?"

All eyes turn toward Grace and me, and I nudge her to answer for us. "Sierra is safe, that's the good news. Jess and I found her outside of Dillon after she escaped from her kidnappers. The bad news is there is still a young girl missing. Sophie, and the kidnappers are using her as leverage against her uncle."

Grace's explanation is brief, but of course, that's not enough information for the BoB group. Questions fly at us, and I say, "Nick and the sheriff's department are assisting the FBI in searching for Sophie. They need volunteers if anyone has time." Several people indicate they'll be joining the search.

"Let's pray for Sophie right now," Kellen suggests, and Pastor Jarrod nods.

"Absolutely."

As the BoB group asks God to protect Sophie and help the authorities find her, I'm encouraged by their faith. When we're finished, I survey the room, studying the faces of my friends. Kellen and Todd sit on either side of Cole, making the floor appear comfortable. Todd's twin, Terri, and their cousin, Macy, are sharing the double recliner, while Caleb perches on the arm of the chair near Macy.

Pastor Jarrod and his wife, Anna, are genuinely caring and always available to talk. Each crisis brings us closer as a group. I've had a deep fear in the pit of my stomach ever since Sierra told us Sophie was still missing. When I think about the prayers that we've lifted for Sophie's safety, a measure of peace settles over me. Sophie is in God's hands, and that's a safe place to be.

11

Sierra

"Honey, could you tell the boys dinner is ready, please?" Aunt Mary bustles around her kitchen, putting the finishing touches on the meal she's been preparing all afternoon.

My lips twitch when I consider calling Uncle Malcolm, Nick, and Levi *boys*. My heart rate increases a little as I slip into the dining room, where they lean over the rectangular table, studying the maps spread out before them.

"Sheriff Herman is leading the grid search near Clark's Lookout, and as soon as we return to Dillon, we can start here." Nick taps his index finger on the map.

I clear my throat and announce, "Dinner is ready." For a second, Uncle Malcom and Nick continue to study the map, but Levi glances up at my words. He nods and continues to watch me with those deep blue eyes. I shuffle self-consciously, and

Uncle Malcolm steps back from the table to come and wrap his arm around my shoulder.

"Hey, sweetheart, how are you feeling?" The tenderness in his voice warms me, but I'm aware of Levi's undisguised concern.

"I'm good, Uncle Mal," I assure him. I'm surprised to catch Levi nodding as if he's also focused on my answer. Uncle Mal guides me toward the kitchen, where the aroma of roasted chicken greets us.

"Did you have a good talk with your mom?" Uncle Mal lowers his voice as he pulls out a chair for me at the kitchen table.

I glance over at my mom and feel combined regret and relief. When I woke from my nap in Piper's room, Mom had been sitting in the rocking chair, watching me. As soon as she saw I was awake, she hurried to the bed and sank down beside me, gathering me close.

Remembering our reunion, I smile. "We talked about a lot of things. Uncle Mal, I'm so sorry I pulled back from everyone the last few weeks. I guess I was testing my independence. I worried Mom, you, and Aunt Mary, even before Clive kidnapped us."

"Honey, it's okay. We understand." My mother slips into the chair beside me and squeezes my hand. "We're so thankful you're safe now." I'm surprised by a tear sliding down her cheek. I was certain she was all cried out by now.

The others take their places at the table, and Uncle Malcolm says grace, asking for God's help in finding Sophie. As soon as he says "Amen," I turn to Nick. "Is there any news?"

Nick spoons mashed potatoes onto his plate as he shakes his head. "We had dogs searching the woods, but they lost the scent, probably where Clive put Sophie in his SUV and drove away."

"How could that be?" I take the bowl of green beans Mom hands me and plop some on my plate. "Sophie could barely walk. He'd have to carry her down the mountain in the dark."

Since Nick is busy chewing, Levi explains, "Turns out, there was an access road about a quarter mile from where you told us you last saw Sophie." He delivers this news carefully as if he's disarming a bomb.

"What?" My fork clatters onto my plate. "Do you mean we hiked all over that mountain when there was a road right there?"

"I'm afraid so," Levi answers. "Clive must be familiar with the area, so he escaped with Sophie." He watches me with genuine regret in his eyes. "I'm sorry."

I take a deep breath, count to ten, and release it with a sigh. "Okay, so what's the next step?"

Nick answers, giving Levi a chance to eat. "We found the cabin," he begins, then holds up his hand as I squeak, "What?"

"Sophie wasn't there." Nick shakes his head, and I recognize the grim determination in his set jaw. "It was empty, but we have our forensics team tearing it apart right now. They'll likely find fingerprints, and if the kidnappers are in the system, we'll be able to ID them."

"And if they aren't in the system?" Aunt Mary asks.

Nick shrugs. "Plan B. Detectives in Missoula are checking on Kemp's known associates. The older woman, Daphne, may be Kemp's girlfriend, for lack of a better term. Once we identify her, it should be easy to find out who Rochelle is."

"Even though you've ID'd Clive, you still won't know where he is," my mom points out. "That poor young girl must be terrified."

My heart aches with the thought of Sophie, alone with the kidnappers, and I push my plate away. "There must be more we can do. Trust me, those three are not criminal masterminds." Something tugs at my memory, and I close my eyes to concentrate. It's right there at the edge of my brain, just out of reach.

"You okay, Sierra?" Mom reaches over and takes my hand.

Poof, it's gone. I turn to give her a soft smile. "I'm good, Mom," I hurry to reassure her. Guilt swamps me as I think of the fear I've caused her with my thoughtlessness.

The lost memory flies by again, taunting me. I'll take time this evening to write what happened from when the kidnappers took us until I saw Jess and Grace on Lover's Leap Road. It's in there, somewhere.

12

Jess

It's wrong somehow that it's such a beautiful day. Often in November we already have snow on the ground, but the temps will hit the mid-forties by this afternoon. The day should be cold and barren, like our hopes of finding Sophie.

Yesterday, I couldn't focus in class, mentally searching every hiding place I could think of around Dillon. And what if they had left the area? I refused to think about that possibility. Besides looking for Sophie, the sheriff's team was also trying to track down Sophie's mom and Uncle Travis.

According to their neighbors, no one had seen them since the day Clive and his posse kidnapped Sophie and Sierra. Nick's frustration is growing, and I whisper a prayer that there will be a break soon.

Pulling Sly's Honda into the parking lot of Justice Savings and Loan, I turn to my passengers. "I need to run in here to cash my paycheck. I should probably get combat pay, since I have to spend time with Amy." A twinge of guilt tries to worm its way into my conscience at my unkind words, but I smother it.

Grace nods without looking up from her phone, and by the smile on her face, I assume she's texting with Kellen.

I take my hand off the door handle as I face Sierra. "Is something wrong?" I ask. Silly question, all kinds of things are wrong. But by Sierra's expression, something new is wrong.

"I just remembered." She points to the sign identifying the building as Justice Savings and Loan. "Right before Sophie and I escaped the cabin, we overheard Clive, Daphne, and Rochelle talking. It sounded like they might have been planning to rob a bank." She points to the sign. "This bank."

"When?" I ask sharply.

Sierra gazes directly at me and replies, "Today."

"OKAY, LET'S TAKE OUR POSITIONS." I lead the way through the side door of Justice Savings and Loan, nodding at Janet Decker, who guards that entrance. And by guard, I mean she sits at a desk looking bored. Janet perks up when she sees us, and I wave.

"Hey, Janet. how are you? We're here to cash my paycheck."

"Wow, that must be some serious money if it takes three of you," Janet jokes.

"If only," I laugh.

We all wave and walk into the lobby of the bank. It's not expansive, but what it lacks in size, it makes up for in architecture. A chandelier hangs from the dome ceiling and sends prisms of light across the marble floor. When I was a little girl, I loved to visit the bank with my parents. I'd imagine I was one of the Bannack prospectors bringing my gold to be stored in the heavy vault. I inhale the musty scent of the old building.

"They're here!" Grace's frantic whisper breaks the spell as Leopard Woman and Rochelle walk through the bank's entrance.

I glance around, hoping to find a good hiding spot where we can watch them while we call for Nick and Levi. I hadn't expected them to arrive so early.

"This way." Grace tugs my arm as she guides Sierra to an alcove off the lobby that leads to a long hallway and the restrooms.

I make sure we're out of sight of our quarry when we enter our hiding spot. A young mom and her daughter pass us on the way to the restroom. The woman gives a curious stare and I grin, then turn to fiddle with the collar of Grace's button-down shirt. "Wardrobe malfunction," I explain. She nods, still looking confused, but smiles as I gripe, "Grace, I can't take you anywhere." They move down the hallway, and I turn to Sierra. "What are they doing now?"

Sierra pokes her head out for a second, and says, "Nothing. Standing by the entrance looking nervous."

Grace slides in beside us in the small space as she pulls at her collar. "You wrinkled my shirt," she complains, but it's a half-hearted gripe.

I mouth *sorry* at her and turn back to study the lobby, where I count seven unsuspecting customers, three bank tellers, and two would-be robbers. I pull my phone from my pocket and prepare to dial Nick. We're simply scouts. Now it's time to call for backup.

"Oh no." If it's possible to whisper and screech at the same time, Sierra rocks it.

I glance up and forget to breathe. Leopard Woman is waving a gun and yelling. "This is a robbery. Everyone on the floor with your heads down." As she turns in our direction, we pull back into our corner, where we hide behind a massive fern that I hope affords us a little extra cover.

"Did she see us?" Grace's voice trembles.

"We'll find out soon enough." Sierra appears to fold in on herself like a caterpillar as she presses against the wall.

"I said, put your heads down!" Leopard Woman's voice

echoes in the lobby. "No one will get hurt if you do what we say." Her voice sounds muffled now, as if she's moved away from us, and I chance a deep breath. It feels so good, I take another.

Glancing down at my phone, I make sure I have Nick's number displayed. I send a text and mute the sound, so notifications are silenced. Then I risk a glance around the corner.

Rochelle is also holding a gun, but it's obvious she doesn't have a clue how to use it, which makes her even more dangerous than Leopard Woman. "I texted Nick," I whisper. "We need to stay quiet, and he'll be here any second."

Sierra holds up her phone and whispers, "I texted Levi, too." Grace and I stare at her until she drops her eyes and shrugs. "What? He gave me his number and told me to contact him if I had any trouble. I think this qualifies."

In the lobby, someone is crying and Leopard Woman snaps, "Shut up. You're getting on my nerves."

I nudge aside a leaf and count the people lying on the floor. Since they dropped right where they stood, they're spread out around the room. An older woman dressed in a gray skirt and cream blazer is curled into a ball, her shoulders shaking as she tries to quiet her sobs. It's Mrs. Metcalf, the school secretary, and my heart aches at her fear. I wish I could somehow signal to her that help is on the way.

I hope.

13

Jess

Rochelle edges toward the wall as if she'd like to disappear through it. Her hand shakes, and as much as I'd like for her to drop the gun, I'm afraid it might go off and shoot someone.

"Grab their cell phones," Leopard Woman snaps at her accomplice. As she approaches a teller window, I'm startled to notice my friend Terri standing on the other side of the counter. Last week Terri told me Mr. Wertz had hired her to work part-time at the bank and she'd be starting on her eighteenth birthday. Today. In fact, Cole and I are going to the twin's party tonight. I hope. I can't tell Todd that bank robbers injured his twin on her first day of work.

"I'm going in," I whisper, and right on cue, Grace grabs my arm and whispers back.

"Nope."

"Look." I nod to where Leopard Woman is standing, waving her gun in Terri's face. Grace's eyes widen and she lets out a tiny screech. Leopard Woman keeps her gun on Terri but swings her head around to stare toward our alcove. I hold my breath and hear tiny sniffles from Grace.

I whisper, "I have to do something," as Leopard Woman turns back to focus on Terri.

Sierra nudges between Grace and me, whispering, "What's happening?"

I nod toward the scene being played out between Terri and Leopard Woman. "It's Terri, from our BoB group."

Sierra's brow furrows, and she whispers. "Oh no. I'm so sorry I got you all involved in this mess."

Grace and I both gape at her. "This isn't on you." Grace offers Sierra a soft squeeze. We all jump when Leopard Woman kicks the front of the counter.

"Hurry," she hisses, and Terri issues a little sob as she shovels the contents of her drawer into a money bag.

I pull away from Grace and Sierra, leaving the cover of the potted plant and slip into the bank lobby. Before Leopard Woman turns in my direction, I flatten myself on the floor and cover my head with my arms, mimicking the other hostages. Maybe she'll think I've been here all along.

A collective gasp echoes when a cell phone rings. Leopard Woman glares at Rochelle. "Turn that thing off."

"I'm trying." Rochelle juggles several cellphones in her hands. One drops to the floor and skitters away, carrying the annoying ring tone with it.

The ringing stops, then a voice announces, "This is Josh. Please leave a message."

We all wait in suspense. Who is interrupting our bank robbery?

A sweet voice coos, "Josh, baby, I hate to fight with you. I'm sorry I said your mother has no taste. I'm sure avocado appliances will come back in style. Eventually. Tell her we'll be happy to give her old refrigerator a new home.

And guess what? My dad heard you wanted to buy a new aluminum fishing boat. And since we're taking our family's junk, um, I mean gifts, my cousin Harvey has an old wooden boat taking up space in the back of his property. Dad dropped it off for you. It has some leaks and rotten places, but you're so handy I'm sure you can fix it up like new. Aren't families amazing? See you soon. Mwah!"

The sound of smacking lips echoes in the taut silence, and I hear a nervous giggle. When Leopard Woman turns my way again, she registers that the noise came from me. She squints in my direction, and I bury my head deeper into my folded arms. The tile floor is hard and cold, but I resist the urge to move. I wish invisibility was my superpower instead of inquisitiveness. *Inquisitivity?* Is that a word?

My inner debate is interrupted when my elbow receives a sharp kick from pointy-toed boots. I grit my teeth and resist the urge to reach out and grab Leopard Woman's ankles and pull her to the floor. She has a gun, and I can't take a chance on it discharging and hurting someone. Maybe me.

"Get up." She kicks my ribs this time. I *oomph* and roll over to glare up at her. "I thought so," she says. "You're that girl from the thrift store the other day."

"Vintage store." I stand to face her.

"Huh?"

Leopard Woman frowns, and I explain, "Verity's Vintage Valuables."

"Whatever." She scrutinizes me. "You're too smart for your own good." I have a flash memory of Nick saying those same words. He didn't mean it as a compliment, either. Nick. Where is he? Leopard Woman reaches around and plucks my phone from my jeans pocket. She opens the phone app and I mentally kick myself for keeping it unlocked.

She scrolls through my phone and locates my last outgoing

call. "Who is Sly?" She doesn't glance up to ask but continues to invade my privacy by opening my texts.

"My sister."

Leopard Woman looks up this time. "Weird name," she says in a judgy tone.

"It's short for Sylvia, which was also my grandmother's name. When I was a baby, I couldn't say *Sylvia*, so I called her Sly. She liked it, and now everyone calls her that." I'm rambling.

She shrugs. "I don't care."

I'm surprised by the flair of anger that surges through me. This woman kidnapped my friend, is holding innocent people hostage, and is pointing a gun at my favorite belly button. But I'm infuriated by her rudeness.

"Ah, did I hurt your feelings, little girl?" She smirks then glances down at the phone screen. "Who is Nick?"

"My brother." It's not a lie, since I'm sure Nick and Sly will be married some day and he will be my brother.

"Hey, knucklehead," Leopard Woman reads out loud. "Party at J S and L. Bring all your friends." I hold my breath as she stares at the message and then continues to scroll.

Sirens break the silence.

Leopard Woman grabs my arm in a painful grip and pulls me over to the window. She chances a quick peek outside and tugs me back against the wall, out of sight of the gathering parade of squad cars and SUVs. She glares at me, and despite my terror, I can't stop myself as I give her a satisfied smile.

"Party time."

14

Jess

Fury flares in Leopard Woman's eyes, and I shrink back. She points the gun at my head. I feel genuine fear.

"Please, God," I whisper, and she scowls, settling her fingers on the trigger of the gun. "Please, God," I repeat the words, and we both jump as the phone in her hand vibrates. She's so startled she drops it to the hard floor, and I have a flash of regret that I didn't add insurance on my phone.

We stare at each other for a moment, then dive for the phone. A loud crack reverberates through the bank lobby as our heads smack together on the way down. Tears blind my eyes, and I feel around on the floor, trying to locate the phone.

My hand touches something hard, and my heart lurches. It's not my phone. It's Leopard Woman's gun. I swipe away tears of pain and pick up the gun, glancing around for her. I'm shocked when I see she's out cold. Nick and Cole always tease me about having a hard head, but yikes!

I scramble to my feet and swing around. Rochelle is watching us, her mouth forming a round *O*. The hand holding her gun trembles and before I can reach her, she drops the gun. As it crashes to the floor, the noise confuses me. Then I understand as intense pain flares through my foot and a bright trickle of blood spreads across the tile floor.

Rochelle shot me in the foot.

From a far distance, I hear shouting. Police officers and FBI agents swarm in, and I glance over at Leopard Woman. Now she's sitting up, shaking her head groggily. I feel intense satisfaction as Nick hauls her up and puts handcuffs on her. His mouth is moving. He must be reciting her Miranda rights.

Fire sears through my foot. Behind me, Grace and Sierra call my name and I glance over my shoulder but they are being held back by officers. I peek down at my left foot, assessing the damage.

I'm not a big fan of blood, especially when it's my own, and the expanding puddle of red is confusing. There must be a lot of blood in my foot. It is ruining my sneaker, and I make a mental note to add Chucks to my Christmas list. A chill races through me, and I shiver. Did someone turn on the AC? Why would they do that in November?

My right foot goes on strike in solidarity with my left. I sway as nausea roils in my stomach. Great, I've been shot, and now I have the flu. As I slide toward the floor, I have the thought, I'm going to miss the twins' birthday party.

Seconds before I hit the floor, strong arms sweep me up. I turn my head and nuzzle my nose into Cole's flannel shirt. He hasn't spoken, but I recognize his scent. Horses, leather, and pine.

"Over here!" His chest rumbles under my cheek when he calls out to the EMTs.

I try to focus on what's happening around me, but the

scorching pain in my foot shoots throbbing fire to my calf. I gasp, and within a few seconds, my tears soak the front of Cole's shirt. He must notice because he bends down to place a gentle kiss on top of my head, murmuring, "I've got you, Jess. I've got you." Cole shifts me in his arms as he lowers me onto a rolling stretcher.

I grab at him. "No."

"It's okay, baby. I'm coming with you."

The stretcher tilts as I'm rolled into the ambulance, but he never lets go of my hand. The nausea returns and I whisper to Cole, "Tell them I think I may have the flu too. I feel kind of sick."

"Shock." Carl, the EMT, bends over me to fix an oxygen mask over my nose.

Groggily, I try to greet him, but all I can say is, "Irgrill."

Carl tosses me a crooked grin. "You should apply for our frequent flyer program. Ride for three, get one free."

Cole grins a little and squeezes my hand. "We'll keep that in mind."

I drift off, thinking what a beautiful word *we* is.

———

AN ANNOYING NOISE WAKES ME, and I swat at the air. "Turn it off," I mumble, keeping my eyes closed. I swing my arm again and plead, "Please, Tweety, five more minutes."

"Tweety?" Carl's voice rumbles above me. "Is that what she calls the sirens?"

"I think that's her alarm clock," Cole explains, and I detect a note of humor in his voice. I don't have to open my eyes to picture him, gray eyes twinkling and a smile tugging at his lips. If Cole is smiling, I must not be dying.

The rest of the day is a kaleidoscope of images. Nurses and doctors surround me on all sides, and then my stretcher is rolling again. As I am taken to the OR, the ceiling tiles move above me.

Someone says, "Remove the bullet." I sure hope I'm allowed to sleep through that part.

Pain pinches the crook of my arm, and I notice a tube extending up to a bag. A nurse with kind eyes leans over me. "Hi Jess. I'm Reya. Dr. Kennedy is going to fix you right up."

I study her face, transfixed by the soft mahogany color of her skin. "You're beautiful," I breathe.

Her brown eyes twinkle. "So are you, honey."

Next comes blessed sleep. When I wake up, it's dark outside. I can make out the outline of the Pioneer Mountains from my bed. A room with a view. I could get used to this, and I drift back to sleep.

15

Sunday
November 17
10:15 a.m.

Jess

"Special delivery!"

I spent a restless night as nurses and orderlies paraded through my room, but none of them had announced themselves like this. I open one eye.

Sly and Maggie enter my hospital room, and I try to scoot up straighter in the bed.

"No, don't move." Sly touches a button on the side of the bed and I'm raised to a sitting position.

Maggie edges forward, never taking her eyes off the tidy white bandage wrapped around my left foot.

"It's okay, Magpie," I assure her. "Gunshots aren't contagious."

"Does it hurt?" Maggie's hazel eyes are glistening, and I want to reassure her.

"It does, but it's getting better."

After the ride in the ambulance—I found out later that Tweety was not there—surgery, recovery, and multiple nurses' visits, I'm pretty much over discussing my foot. I watch as Sly lifts the lid from a plastic container to reveal chocolate chip cookies. When I reach for one, I discover they're still warm. "I love you," I tell Sly.

"Same." She gives me a gentle smile.

"Hey, what about me?" Maggie reaches for a cookie. "I helped."

Sly and I grin at each other, and say together, "It's Shake 'n Bake, and I helped!" For a moment, we're all back in our kitchen, where Daddy and Mama are making chili. Daddy didn't cook much. Mamma always said her gift was preparation and his gift was consumption. But when he assisted in the kitchen, he always quoted the famous commercial. Ironically, I don't remember Mamma ever using the product Shake 'n Bake.

I let the homemade goodness of the cookie fortify me, then ask, "How bad is it?" At my question, we all three stare at the white bandage wrapped around my left foot.

"Well, in the world of gunshot wounds," Sly begins, but Maggie interrupts her.

"GSW," Maggie corrects, solemnly.

Sly nods. "Yes, GSW." Weirdly, my foot throbs, as if it understands we're talking about it. "Dr. Kennedy said you were very fortunate," Sly continues. "In several ways. First, the bullet was a .22, the smallest caliber of bullet. It entered and exited your foot at what they call Zone 2 and missed all twenty-six bones in your foot. They cleaned and bandaged it and put on a soft cast. He says within a month you should be able to do everything but pole vault."

"But Jess can't pole vault." Maggie is confused.

"Precisely." Sly grins. She inherited Daddy's sense of humor. Unexpected tears sting my eyes at the thought of Mamma and Daddy again. I wish they were here. They are having a great time in Heaven, but I need them. We need them.

Sudden waves of exhaustion sweep through me, and I slide down into the bed. My eyelids are heavy, so I give in and close them. Sly smooths my hair away from my face, then she leans down and whispers, "I miss them too." My sisters walk to the door as sleep starts to claim me.

A panicked thought makes my eyelids fly up again. "Leave the cookies!"

16

Sunday
November 17
10:30 a.m.

Sierra

I scan the sanctuary of the church, recognizing several people. Mom and I always visit Cornerstone Community Church when we're at Uncle Mal's. At college in Missoula, I attend a campus church that meets in a three-story Victorian house where several girls live during the school year. I enjoy the relaxed atmosphere, but I've missed the worship band and the sound of many voices singing together. I'm glad I have both opportunities.

The McBride clan almost takes up an entire row in the sanctuary. We've settled into our seats when I feel someone sit next to me. I turn with a smile, expecting Sly or Maggie, but my smile fades when I see Deputy Levi Cooper.

"Those seats are for Sly and Maggie," I say.

"No, they're not," Levi says with haughty confidence.

I narrow my eyes and glare at him. "Yes," I say through gritted teeth, "they are."

I catch a twinkle in his eyes when he leans over to whisper, "Nick told me they went to the first service so they could visit Jess before we eat dinner."

I frown. "*We* eat dinner?"

"Yes, Nick invited me to join you all after church. I'm sorry, though, that I won't be there long, since I'll need to relieve Nick."

I'm puzzled by the *I'm sorry* statement. Is he sorry he can't stay, or does he think I'm sorry he can't stay? Not likely. The seat on the other side of Levi is empty. I open my mouth to suggest he scoot over so he can be more comfortable. Before I can utter a word, Mrs. Hanover settles into the seat and removes that option.

Levi delivers a grin that seems to say, "Winning!" But a moment later, his nose wrinkles and he sneezes. I turn away and hide my smile. Mrs. Hanover has a new perfume.

At dinner, Levi has changed from his church clothes into his uniform. I'm sure he was happy to make the switch. Even so, I hide a grin when Aunt Mary leans over during dinner and takes a delicate sniff.

"New cologne, Levi?" she asks.

Before he can respond, Uncle Mal and Cole say together, "Mrs. Hanover."

"Ah." Aunt Mary nods in understanding. "That would do it."

I was a little sorry for Levi when he sneezed three times at church. Allergies are miserable. But after that first reaction, he seemed fine. Just fragrant.

I fake a cough to camouflage a giggle. Levi is watching me from his place next to Aunt Mary, and his serious expression makes me feel guilty for laughing at his predicament. My grin fades and I'm practicing my apology when he winks at me. Winks! I glance around the table to check if anyone noticed, but they all seem focused on Aunt Mary's pot roast.

I study my plate, a flush heating my cheeks. A few moments later, when Levi excuses himself to leave for his shift, I feel sort of let down. I shake myself a little then stand and pick up my plate. Next, I reach for Cole's plate, but I'm stopped by the sight of his fork hovering over my hand.

"Don't even think about it," he warns, and I step back. Around the table, everyone else is still busy eating.

Flushing, I consider sitting back down to finish my dinner. Instead, I say, "It's all delicious, Aunt Mary, but I guess I'm still a little rattled from yesterday. Would it be okay if I covered my plate with foil and put it in the fridge for later?"

"Of course, sweetheart."

As I walk behind Cole's chair, I hear him mutter, "Just because Levi left doesn't mean dinner is over."

I wander through Uncle Mal's sprawling house and look out the large windows of the sunroom, to see a light snowfall. Snow. I hadn't considered that. Is Sophie's yellow sweater warm enough? I hope Clive isn't hauling her all over the mountains in this weather.

Uncle Mal pops his head into the living room, where I've been pacing a pattern on the carpet. "Your ride is here."

"Huh?" My confusion ends when I notice Grace peeking around him.

"Hi, I thought we could ride to the hospital together," she offers.

My restlessness evaporates with the thought of action. I grab my jacket from the hook near the front door. "Let's go."

Grace smiles in understanding, and within minutes we are joining the light traffic heading to the outskirts of Dillon. "I thought you might go a little stir-crazy," Grace explains as she pulls into the hospital parking lot. "Besides, this is where all the action is today."

In a few minutes, I understand Grace's comment as we near Jess's hospital room. A low rumble of conversation and laughter comes from beyond the open door. We enter to an obvious breach of hospital protocol. Six visitors fill the room, double the amount allowed at one time.

Cole sits next to Jess, their hands entwined on top of the blanket. Half of the BoB youth group is filling every empty spot in the room. Terri is arranging golden mums and yellow sunflowers in a vase. Grace's boyfriend, Kellen, and Terri's twin, Todd, are adjusting the angle of the television that hangs high in a corner.

Two hand-drawn pictures are in a place of honor taped to a bulletin board. One might be a vase of flowers. A dash of color brightens the picture, and Janey's name is printed on the bottom of the page. Joey's name is scrawled across the top of the second picture, which features a black squiggly *S* with a vertical line drawn through it. I think it is supposed to be a dollar sign.

I'm puzzled for a second, then realize it could represent a bank. Underneath the dollar sign is another drawing of what appears to be a rocket launcher. It's hard to tell for sure since Joey partially erased the picture. I can imagine the conversation when he showed the rocket launcher picture to his mom.

Pastor Jarrod and Anna stand at the head of the bed, talking to Jess and Cole. Kellen notices us first, since he must have Grace radar. He hurries over to take the basket of muffins Grace is carrying.

She grins and teases, "These are for Jess."

"Of course." Kellen looks wounded. "I'll guard them with my life."

"*Hmm.*" Grace looks doubtful as Kellen walks back to Todd, placing the basket on a nearby table. "Watch them," she mutters to me as we approach Jess's bedside.

We share greetings while Jess stares with too-bright eyes. I glance at Cole, speculating at the furrowing in his forehead. He's worried about something.

"Jess, we're going to take off now," Pastor Jarrod says as Anna pats Jess's shoulder. "We're all praying for you, although from the doctor's report, it sounds like God's already on the job."

Grace and I step aside as the couple leaves, nodding our agreement to their instruction to "take care of our girl."

Grace leans down and places a soft kiss on Jess's head. "Hey, friend," she says, and a tear sparkles in her eyes.

At dinner today, we discussed how trauma affects people in different ways and times. "Keep it in mind when you visit Jess," Aunt Mary had told us. "She'll try to dismiss the trauma. She can make all the jokes she wants about being shot in the foot, but it's not a joke. And it will take more than a bandage to address her injuries, physical and emotional."

I think about my aunt's words now as I watch Jess brush away those quick tears and smile at Grace with mischief. "Just call me Hopalong." Everyone laughs, but Cole's mouth tightens, and I bet he's remembering his mom's words, too.

Nurse Reya bustles in, carrying an ear thermometer. She observes the crowded room. "Hey, girlie, quick temp check." Grace and I step back, and she glides up to the bed and uses the ear thermometer. She frowns as she touches Jess's forehead. "How are you feeling, honey?"

Jess's smile appears a little forced. "Great. Dr. Kennedy said I can go home tomorrow morning."

"*Hmm*," is the nurse's noncommittal response as she and Cole share a meaningful look.

"Hey, guys," Cole says, addressing all of us. "Thanks for all the flowers and treats, but Jess should rest now." His tone is kind but firm. Jess opens her mouth, likely to protest, but I notice Cole rub his thumb up and down the top of her hand that is held in his. Soothing her.

Jess leans back with a trembling smile and says, "Thanks, everyone. Love you all," and closes her eyes. We all leave, but I'm curious when Cole stops at the nurse's station for a quiet conversation with Nurse Reya. Concern settles in my stomach as I follow my friends outside.

17

Sierra

I n the parking lot, we scatter to our cars, with Kellen joining Grace and me for the ride back to the McBride house. Kellen starts to climb into the backseat, but I shake my head and slide in there instead. Kellen shares a quick smile and I understand why Grace likes him so much.

Nick's squad car is parked in the driveway, so we all hurry inside, eager for any news about Sophie. We enter through the back door into the spacious kitchen and discover dinner leftovers on the sideboard.

Aunt Mary comes into the room. "Help yourselves to anything out here, but we ordered some pizzas too. Nick is about to give us an update on the two bank robbers."

I grab one of Aunt Mary's famous biscuits off a tray and make my way to the dining room. Behind me, Grace says, "Thanks,

Mrs. McBride. Kellen and I have dinner plans, but we would like to hear Nick's report."

Settling into a chair, I reach for the butter that is always present on my aunt's table. I butter the biscuit and take a bite, closing my eyes in appreciation. *Mmm*, there is something to be said for comfort food. I open my eyes to catch everyone watching me. "What?" I shrug. "It's good."

Nick clears his throat, and I'm relieved when everyone's focus turns to him. I'm a bit surprised at the disappointment I feel when I don't see Deputy Cooper at the table. No, I'm not disappointed, I correct myself. I'm relieved he's out there, still searching for Sophie.

"We've charged the two women with attempted bank robbery and assault with a deadly weapon," Nick begins, then he turns to me. "Sierra, I'll need you to come down to the Sheriff's office tomorrow for a formal identification, and we'll add kidnapping charges."

I nod, the biscuit dry in my mouth. I need more butter.

"Daphne and Rochelle met in prison, where they both served time for theft. They were released around the same time, and when Daphne reconnected with Clive, she brought Rochelle along." Nick takes a long swig of his sweet tea and continues. "We found your car, Sierra, parked a few blocks from the bank. When the techs finish processing it, you can have it back."

Although I'm grateful my car has survived Daphne and Rochelle, I focus on the most important question. "Sophie?"

Nick shakes his head, and he hesitates in telling me the next part. "The women say they haven't contacted Kemp since the morning you and Sophie escaped. He told them to clear out anything in the cabin that could identify them and said he'd send a message about where to meet after they robbed the bank. They took off in your car, Sierra, and haven't heard from him since."

"But they could be lying," I protest.

Nick nods. "Could be. But we offered them some good terms

if they gave us info to help find Sophie. They have no incentive to lie."

I slump back in my chair. "Sophie's gone."

Nick's frown is sharp, as if he takes exception to my words and defeated tone. "We don't have her yet, but we will."

Grace comes over and wraps one arm around my shoulder. "But God," she whispers.

Her words bring a flicker of hope, even as a knot of sick dread forms in the pit of my stomach. I'm aware of Grace and Kellen leaving for their dinner date, but I can't seem to rouse myself to say goodbye.

Staring down at my lap, I'm startled when Nick is beside me, kneeling next to my chair. "Sierra," he says, and now I'm talking to my cousin and not the deputy sheriff.

"We will find her," he repeats. "Have faith, if not in me, then in God. He loves Sophie even more than you do. We've asked Him to protect her, and I believe He will."

I turn and wrap my arms around his shoulders, and I'm sure my few tears are tickling his neck. After a second, I feel a light pat on my head and smile. Poor Nick. He's not very demonstrative, except with Sly. I kind of ambushed him.

"Pizza delivery!"

Nick stands and walks back to his chair. I swipe a few stray tears away and look up to discover Deputy Cooper, holding two enormous pizza boxes. His eyes focus on me as Uncle Mal takes the pizza from him. The conversation flows around us, but it feels like we're the only two people in the room.

I'm surprised at the compassion I discern in his blue eyes. He must have arrived right in time to catch me crying on Nick's shoulder. Literally. He gives me a brief nod, but it feels like there is a wealth of meaning in the gesture, and I have the sense that he's trying to reassure me, just as Nick had.

BY EIGHT O'CLOCK GRACE RETURNS, and we take two blankets out to the enclosed porch. A small electric heater sits in a corner between two overstuffed chairs. We settle in to wait for a report from Sly. She'd told Grace she was going to drop Maggie at Rachel's house to spend the night. Then she would return to the hospital to check on Jess. We're all hoping the doctor releases Jess tomorrow to begin her recovery at home.

I wrap my hands around my mug of tea, hoping some warmth will seep in. Grace snuggles down in her blanket. She's staring out the multi-paned window, studying the darkness on the other side.

"Grace?" She doesn't respond, and I reach over to touch her arm, which is cocooned in the blanket. "Grace?"

She focuses on my face, and I'm startled by the tears meandering through her light freckles.

"Do you think we messed up?" Grace's gaze is intense. "At the bank, I mean. We should have called Nick right away and stayed in the car until he arrived." She nibbles her lower lip with such intensity I'm concerned she'll draw blood.

"Hey," I say. "We couldn't be sure the women were going to show up. Nick was in the middle of the search for Sophie, and we didn't want to distract him for a wild goose chase, remember?" My lip stings, and I realize I'm imitating Grace's lip nibbling. I've struggled with this question myself. My mom sometimes says, "Hindsight is 20/20," and I'm sure that's never been more true than in this case.

"Jess texted Nick as soon as they showed up," Grace reasons. "And one of the FBI agents said the response time was seven minutes. Even if we texted Nick when we were in the car, he'd only have about two extra minutes to get there."

I nod, but we're both silent as we consider what happened during those last two minutes before the authorities arrived. Rochelle shot Jess. We both nibble again.

I break the silence with a sudden thought. "Speaking of texting Nick, do you have any idea why Jess sent him such a weird message? She could have said, 'Bank robbery, hurry, please.' I mean, it got the job done, but why did she call him a knucklehead? Who even uses that term?" I'm relieved by the twitch of a smile on Grace's lips.

"Nick asked Jess the same question. Jess explained she's always mad at people on television shows who send obvious texts that the bad guy can understand. So, she made it sound like a party invitation." Grace smiles, obviously impressed by Jess's cunning.

"And the knucklehead part?" I ask.

"Yeah, Sly said Nick was curious about that too." Grace grins. "Jess said she wanted to grab Nick's attention, and she thought that would do it."

I laugh at the image of Nick reading the text while he's surrounded by FBI agents. Jess is a genius, and I'm eager to have her back with us.

Grace appears to be calmer now. I sip my tea, while flashes of yesterday's events flit through my mind. The sound of a car door shutting brings me out of my thoughts, and Grace and I jump up to meet Sly at the door.

Sly sways, and I reach for her. My heart aches, as I imagine what it must be like to carry the weight of all the trauma the Thomas sisters have endured in such a short time. "Sly, would you like some hot tea or cocoa?" I offer, drawing her into the warmth of the room.

She shakes her head. "I can't stay. But I need to talk to you all."

Alarm skitters through me at her words and the concern clouding her eyes. "Of course." I lead the way to the living room where my mom, Uncle Mal, Aunt Mary, and Cole are sitting.

When Cole spots Sly, he stands and asks, "How is she?"

Sly's dark eyes glisten with unshed tears. "Not good. Dr. Kennedy says the gunshot wound has caused an infection. When the bullet passed through her foot, it carried tiny pieces of her shoe and dirt."

"But I thought that's what the surgery was for, to do debridement and make sure everything was clean inside." Aunt Mary's voice trembles a little as she reaches out to take Uncle Mal's hand.

"Yes, but they said there is always a possibility of infection, especially in a close-up gunshot wound." Sly slumps onto the loveseat, and Grace hurries to settle next to her, wrapping an arm around her shoulders.

"So, Jess can't come home tomorrow?" Grace asks.

Sly shakes her head, then says in a wavering voice, "Her fever is almost a hundred and four. Dr. Kennedy said they consider that dangerous. I'm afraid our Jess won't be coming home anytime soon."

18

Jess

"Sly, check the stove. Something's burning." I roll my head back and forth on the pillow, trying to find a cool spot. That's a fail.

"You are." I recognize Cole's voice, but someone must have glued my eyelids closed. I can't open them. This is a shame because I am desperate to see his face. I can picture his gray eyes, which I feel focused on me. He may have some stubble. I sigh. I like his stubble. Sudden panic sweeps through me and I say, "G'way."

Confusion sounds in his voice. "You want me to leave?"

I try to swallow but my mouth feels like it is full of cotton balls. Something cold touches my lips and I open them to take in the ice chips. "G'way," I repeat. "I'm ugly." I could phrase it better, but my mind has a limited vocabulary right now.

Cole runs his thumb over the top of my hand in that soothing gesture he uses to calm me. "No, you're beautiful."

Tears sting my eyes, but all I can say is, "Okay," and I'm dreaming again.

At first, the sand is warm as I try to get comfortable on my beach towel. But soon the heat scorches and engulfs me. I thrash around, trying to find a cool spot, but I'm so weak I can scarcely move. Every part of my body hurts. This is the worst vacation ever.

Later, I'm dimly aware the room is full of people. I squint my eyes open and find Pastor Jeff, Pastor Jarrod, Sly, and Mr. and Mrs. McBride standing near me. For a second, I'm confused about why they're here. Actually, why am I here? The answer comes when I close my eyes again.

I'm dying. I'm sad about that, but when I think about seeing Mamma and Daddy my heart leaps. Somewhere in my mind, a voice whispers, "But God."

The next time I surface, I'm aware of Sly and Maggie talking near my bedside.

"Sly, we can't lose Jess too." My heart hurts at the pain in Maggie's voice. At thirteen, Maggie has already been through more than any child should have to face. Losing our parents in that terrible car crash nearly broke us all.

"Magpie." Sly's soft voice is barely audible. I wish they'd speak up. I try to open my mouth to make the request, but nothing happens. If I could talk, I'd tell them I'm ready to leave the beach. I can't imagine the sunburn I'll have after sleeping so long on the scorching sand.

The last beach trip we took was in eighth grade, when our family vacationed in Florida. I remember how comforting and warm the sun felt on my skin. But now something is wrong. The sun is blazing down on me, and I feel like I'm under a heavy blanket. I've never felt so hot, and I want to move and escape the scorching heat, but every single cell in my body hurts. I give this vacation zero stars.

I'm about to drift off when a deep voice says, "Sly, may I speak with you, please?"

A chair scrapes the floor, and Maggie says, "No, Sly, don't leave. I want to hear what Dr. Kennedy says. Jess is my sister, too, and I deserve to know." I'm surprised and a little proud of the determination in Maggie's voice. Wait, they are going to talk about me. I hope they let me stay for the conversation too.

"We are concerned that Jess's fever is climbing, rather than declining." Dr. Kennedy sounds nice. I hope I'm able to meet him someday.

"We thought the new antibiotic would deal with the B. cereus pathogen that is attacking her body. Instead, her fever is nearing 106. Organ failure, particularly her liver, is our greatest concern now." I hear a gasp but can't determine which sister reacted. I'd gasp, too, but I'm exhausted.

"What?" Sly begins, then clears her throat. "What is the plan?"

"We're going to increase the antibiotic and pray we can bring the fever down soon. The nurses will continue to give Jess cool sponge baths. If her temp climbs any more, we'll need to transfer her to our intensive care unit and begin ice baths."

I recognize Maggie's smothered sob.

"What can we do?" Sly asks.

"Just keep praying." Dr. Kennedy says.

The beach is calling, and I have to leave. As I drift away, I'm sure I hear my mother's voice, saying, "But, God."

19

Tuesday
November 19
6:00 p.m.

Sierra

I'm laying out paper plates around the dining table when the kitchen door opens and slams shut. That poor door has been getting a real workout. Aunt Mary's dining room has become command central with a steady stream of people during the day and evening. Sly and Maggie have been eating all their meals here so they can be at the hospital as much as possible.

This morning, Sly encouraged Maggie to go back to school, hoping to distract her from Jess's illness. Maggie lasted until noon, when she called for a ride and I borrowed Aunt Mary's car to pick her up.

We stopped by the hospital, only to be told there was no change. We stayed with Jess while Sly slipped away for a meal and a fifteen-minute nap. When she returned, Nick was with her, and I grilled him on the search for Sophie. It took all my self-control not to yell at him when he said there was no new information.

By the time Maggie and I left the hospital, school was out so we stopped to pick up Rachel, and I dropped the girls at Rachel's house.

Her parents have been wonderful, keeping Maggie overnight so Sly can be available to go to the hospital. So many families have stepped in to help, especially with food.

Nick and Sheriff Herman often stop for a quick bite before returning to the search. The Ellison family dropped off an enormous pot of chili for tonight's meal, along with two dozen cornbread muffins. Grace's mom contributed a huge lasagna last night, along with the most delicious brownies I've ever tasted.

And this morning, Mrs. Mendelssohn brought over something she called a breakfast casserole, telling Mom it had a secret ingredient no one would ever guess. Mrs. Mendelssohn is famous for entering her concoctions, as Uncle Mal calls them, into cooking contests.

As far as I'm aware, she's never won, but last year she received an award from one contest. They recognized her for the most submissions to the contest through the years. The award said 'retired' on it, and Mrs. M. is very proud of it. Uncle Mal jokes it's their nice way of trying to tell her not to send any more entries. But I'm sure that won't stop her.

The BoB youth group stopped by this afternoon to drop off soda, sweet tea, and chips. Pastor Jarrod called us all together in a circle to pray for Jess and Sophie. After everyone left, I noticed a growing frustration in myself. I've always believed in the power of prayer. Although my relationship with God is a little wobbly at the moment, I know He loves us. But I'd appreciate a little action on His part about now.

I open the five-pound bag of ice the BoB group brought and pour it into an oversized bowl. A few cubes land gracefully, then a massive chunk of ice ruins the effect with a loud clatter. Sighing, I take the ice pick I've brought along and start stabbing.

With every minute, the frustration bubbles up higher and higher. Sophie's been alone with Clive for almost a week now. Nick and the FBI have tried everything to find them, including search dogs. There's no sign of her.

I would give anything to go back to that moment on the mountain, when Clive took Sophie. I should have tried to find them, although I couldn't see which direction he took her. But I'd figured as soon as I alerted the authorities, they would track down Clive and we'd have Sophie safe at home by nightfall. Although, considering what Sophie told me about her home life, *safe* doesn't seem like an option.

"Are you okay?" I jump at the sound of Cole's voice and he studies me with concern.

Immediately, I feel bad for letting my emotions overwhelm me. Cole is exhausted, his eyelids heavy with fatigue. He's been at the hospital almost all day. As a senior, he can't afford to miss much school, and I'm sure he's already falling behind. At least Bob Hadley has been very understanding about him needing time off.

Cole mentioned to Aunt Mary that Amy Sinclair is helping out at the stables to give him time with Jess. I'm not sure how I feel about that fact, given Amy's past antagonism toward Jess, but I try to give Amy the benefit of the doubt. Maybe she has had a change of heart. Jess works at the stable, too, and I spotted a new arrangement of flowers from Hadley Ranch when I visited earlier.

"I'm fine." I try to make my smile not resemble a snarl, but Cole appears unconvinced.

He walks over to take the ice pick. "I think it's dead, Jim."

I'm surprised into a laugh at the Star Trek reference, then sober and ask, "Any news on Jess?" I left the hospital three hours ago and need hope.

Cole clears his throat. "No. They're trying a new antibiotic since the others haven't seemed to work. At one point, her temperature came down to 102, but then it shot back up to 105."

Cole looks at me, and I've never seen my cousin so vulnerable before. "Sierra, she's really sick."

I move over to wrap my arms around his waist. "She'll be okay, Cole. She has to be." I wince at my words. Wishing won't make it so.

Cole's voice is hoarse when he says, "Yes, I'm trusting God to make that happen."

I grit my teeth to keep from demanding, "So why doesn't He do something?" Instead, I hug Cole. "We're all praying." That's not a lie. I joined the BoB prayer group thirty minutes ago, holding hands with Macy and Terri. I prayed. I'm just not sure I believe.

We turn at the sound of voices coming from the kitchen. Cole leaves to greet the newcomers, but I stay to assassinate the ice a little longer. With every strike, my anger returns, hotter and hotter. Patience isn't one of my strengths, and worrying about Sophie and Jess has taken me to the edge.

"Sierra," Mom calls from the kitchen, and I try to calm myself. I need to help feed the search volunteers that have arrived. Ice pick in hand, I walk into the kitchen and immediately see him. Deputy Levi Cooper. In my mind, the name drips with sarcasm. I haven't seen him in two days, since he's been busy with the search for Sophie. But that's not enough. If he's such an outstanding soldier and cop, why hasn't he found her yet?

For a moment I feel like I'm split into two people. Good Sierra understands Levi has worked hard, even taking on longer shifts to give Nick a chance to be with Sly at the hospital. He doesn't deserve my anger. Bad Sierra sees red. How dare he come here and eat while Sophie is missing?

As I enter the room, Levi lifts a plastic cup to his lips to drink as he laughs at a comment from Uncle Mal. Now he's laughing? Good Sierra whispers in my ear, "You're projecting your frustration onto Levi. You're scared, angry, and hormonal. This will not end well." Bad Sierra stabs Good Sierra with the ice pick.

"What are you doing here?" I practically snarl, not recognizing my voice.

Levi pauses with the cup halfway to his lips. I catch a flicker of ... something ... in his blue eyes. Surprise, hurt, anger, sympathy? All the above?

"Sierra!" Reproach tints Mom's voice, but that's all she says. I must have shocked her into speechlessness. All other conversations have stopped as everyone watches the drama.

Levi places his cup on the sideboard and says evenly, "Nick invited me to grab some dinner before I go back to the search." He's watching me like you'd watch a wild animal, calm but ready for action if needed.

"Well, I hope Sophie gets to have some dinner tonight too. Do you understand what terrible things could be happening to her right now?"

"I'm aware." Levi's voice carries a wealth of knowledge that suggests, 'I've seen things I pray you never have to see.'

"Then go find her," I yell. Cole removes the ice pick from my fingers, but no one speaks. Levi moves out of the room. Swinging around, I hurry after him through the dining room and into the living room. I'm surprised to find Nick and Sly sitting close on the loveseat. I startle them, too, and I register the confusion on Sly's face.

Nick's focus goes to Levi, and he raises a dark eyebrow then nods. At Levi.

"Excuse us," Levi firmly takes my hand and tugs me toward the closed-in porch. Sly opens her mouth to say something, but Nick whispers in her ear and she examines me curiously.

I lift my chin and say, "Yes, let's talk," as if it's all my idea. I'm not sure what I expect. It's not like he can arrest me for rudeness. In the short time I've known Deputy Levi Cooper, I feel like I've learned how to read him, at least a little. Now emotions play across his features as I assume he considers what to do with me. I step back as I identify what I imagine is his temptation for an angry kiss.

My heart races. I lick my lips and he watches, anger simmering in those blue eyes. Then he stuns me by grinning.

"Oh no, sweetheart," he drawls. "Not yet. That's not how this is going to go."

I have the weirdest feeling he's not just talking about this moment. At what I assume is my confused expression, Levi smiles, and the rest of the anger drains from his eyes. I'm relieved, but when compassion replaces the anger, I take another step backward. Levi advances and now I'm standing with my back to the wall. He's not crowding me, and now, instead of feeling threatened, I feel comforted.

"It's been a terrible week for you, hasn't it?" The words are simple, but the concern on his face makes me look away as tears threaten. I lose that battle and soon they are falling, faster and faster. In fact, I think I hear a tiny sob in there. "Can I hold you?" Levi's words are more than a polite request. I sense that if I say yes, my whole life will change.

I nod but Levi says, "I need the word, honey."

My throat is thick with tears, but I squeak out, "Yes."

Slowly, he draws me into his arms and stands there, holding me. I sniffle and try to compose myself, but Levi says, "It's okay, Sierra. Cry." So I do.

Later, I'm aware of voices coming from the driveway as people leave for either the hospital or to join the search. I tense, realizing we're visible through the porch windows. Without a word, Levi leads me over to one of the big chairs. I sit, and he crouches down in front of me.

"I need to go," he says, and I'm overwhelmed by guilt.

"But you didn't eat your dinner," I wail.

He grins. "I'll take something to go." He studies me for a moment. "Are you okay, now?"

I nod, a flush rising in my cheeks, as I remember what I said to him. In front of everyone! "I'm sorry," I begin, but he shakes his head.

"God's got this, Sierra," he says with a certainty I wish I felt. "Trust Him. Trust me." Then he disappears into the night.

I sit down in Aunt Mary's rocker and consider what just happened. What *is* happening? I thought I'd built an unshakable defense against Levi. I touch the dog tags tucked under my sweater. They're supposed to be a reminder of how much it hurts to lose someone. But each time I'm with Levi, that reminder becomes more about love and not loss.

As devastating as my dad's death was to us, Mom and I are thankful for every single day we had with him. I sit there for a long time, contemplating if some things are worth taking the risk.

Later, I enter the kitchen and join Mom, Aunt Mary, and Sly as they clean up from the come-and-go dinner. I take a deep breath and say, "I'm sorry."

"Not us you owe the apology," Mom snaps as she places leftovers in the fridge. I recognize that tone. She's embarrassed.

I walk to my mom and hug her. "I am sorry," I repeat. "And I apologized to Levi." It feels weird to say his name and a flush stains my cheeks again. At this rate, everyone will think I'm sunburned.

Mom sniffs, and I feel her relax a little, but she's not quite done. "What were you thinking, girl?" she demands. "You realize that man carries a gun, don't you?" Snickers come from Aunt Mary and Sly.

"I'm aware," I say, mimicking one of Levi's favorite phrases. Aunt Mary and Sly glance at each other and snicker louder. "What?" I ask.

They laugh harder, and my heart lightens. The whole evening

was worth it, just to hear Sly laugh. I'm glad I could do my part. I grab a mysterious rust-colored cookie and head to the living room.

In the background, Sly calls out, "Mrs. Mendelssohn alert!" I consider the cookie and decide to risk it.

20

Wednesday
November 20
_11:00 a.m._

Jess

My heart pounds as I race through the night, the moonlight illuminating the shadowed buildings. I stumble over something and try to keep my balance. If I fall, I'm dead.

The outline of the visitor's center looms, and I hope the back door is unlocked. The caretakers of Bannack are very conscientious, though, so it's not likely. No time to check. Outlaw is panting behind me, and I try to run faster. I'm so weak. My feet feel like I have dead weights attached, and each breath is becoming more labored.

I've been running from this cougar for hours, and while I'm about to drop, he gains momentum. Turning a corner, I'm on the main street of Bannack. Not a street really, more a worn path between the old buildings. In the distance, I notice a group of people, and my heart leaps as I recognize Nick, Cole, Sly, and

Grace. I gather all my strength and yell as loud as I can, "Outlaw is in Bannack!"

"Jess, wake up." Gentle hands touch my shoulder, but the words are urgent. I shake my head back and forth so violently that I expect my long hair to fly around my face. But I feel a soft pillow underneath my cheek as I turn and slowly open my eyes.

"Jess." My name sounds like a whispered prayer. I blink several times, trying to focus on Cole's tortured expression.

"Cole?" I whisper and squeeze my eyes shut as pain pounds through my head. I'm aware of my parched throat and try to swallow.

"Here." Cole places an ice chip on my lips, and I greedily take it.

"More," I croak, and he complies. I gather my strength to open my eyes again, and I'm shocked to discover tears gleaming in Cole's gray eyes. Panic races through me. Cole never cries, at least never in front of me. Not even when Outlaw attacked Roxie, Cole's beloved dog, last month.

"Who's dead?" I whisper and startle a strained chuckle from Cole.

"No one." Determination in his voice contrasts with the tears rolling down his cheeks into his unshaven beard. I'm kind of a connoisseur of Cole's stubble, so I estimate he hasn't shaved in at least four days. Is he doing No Shave November?

He leans over to kiss my forehead, and he whispers, "You're still burning up. I'll find the doctor."

My eyelids close, and as much as I'd like to continue our conversation, I drift away.

I DREAM Cole is sitting next to me, holding my hand.

"I love you," he says. "Please don't leave me."

I struggle to abandon the beach, longing for his strong arms. "I love you, too," I say, but I'm afraid he doesn't hear me.

An annoying beep wakes me, and I mumble, "Sly, the microwave is done. I'm cooked." Funny to be cooked in a microwave, but I must be, from the terrible heat I've been soaking up.

"Jess?" Cole's voice sounds groggy, and I open my eyes. He's slumped in a chair beside my bed.

"Hi, you," I croak. "I was at the beach."

Cole stands and leans over to touch my face. "Welcome home."

"I think I went swimming." I try to explain why my face is wet. In fact, my whole body feels soaked, and I shiver a little.

Cole makes a sound between a laugh and a sob, then stands. "Where's Dr. Kennedy? Your fever broke!"

Broken is rarely a good thing, but Cole is happy, so I don't worry about it. Beach time is over, and I slip into a sweet sleep.

21

Sierra

I sit at Aunt Mary's kitchen table, cutting homemade noodles for tonight's dinner. With all the time I've spent in the kitchen this week, maybe I should consider becoming a chef.

I enjoy rolling the pizza cutter along the big slab of dough. I'm tempted to sample the dough, but Mom stops by the table and warns, "Don't even try it. There's raw egg in that dough."

She moves on to the pantry and returns with a granola bar, which she places next to my elbow. Without another word, she returns to the sink, where she and Aunt Mary are washing up the lunch dishes. I'd hoped Levi would stop by for lunch today, but Nick mentioned to Aunt Mary that Levi was leading a search party in the Blacktail Mountains.

"Dan Stafford offered to let them use his hunting cabin as a command center, so they'll be gone a couple of days, assuming they don't find Sophie before that."

Sighing, I sneak a raw noodle. At least I'm useful by helping Aunt Mary and Mom with the food prep for the volunteers, but I'm getting restless. I want to join the search for Sophie. Maybe it will help distract me from my worry over Jess. After a lot of discussion, Mom and I agreed that I will wait until January to return to school. I'd be worthless in my classes, longing to be here for Sophie and Jess. Coach Dwyer has been very understanding and promised my position on the volleyball team will be waiting for me when I return.

Last evening, Sly and Maggie stopped by for dinner, but neither one seemed to touch Aunt Mary's famous lasagna. Apparently, Dr. Kennedy said if Jess didn't improve soon, they'd have to move her to the ICU. Something about the effects of a high fever on her liver.

Tears sting my eyes as I slice through the noodles. I need to get out of here. Maybe Cole will take me to Hadley's today. I dream of flying across the field on Chieftain's back. That probably won't happen, but I can exercise Daisy, since Jess hasn't been able to work.

Guilt swamps me. Jess is fighting for her life right now, and I'm thinking of racing away on her favorite horse. Some friend I am. The kitchen door opens, and Cole walks in. I hop up to ask him if I can go to Hadley's. I'll deal with my guilt later. Right now, I have to escape.

"Cole?" Aunt Mary's voice holds a tinge of fear as she turns to her son. He appears to be in shock, and his reddened eyes make it obvious tears have fallen at some point.

"Her fever broke. Jess will be okay."

Aunt Mary releases an excited cry and hurries to wrap him in a hug. "Tell us everything," she encourages.

And he does.

22

Sierra

With Jess out of danger, everyone's focus centers on Sophie again. The next two days pass with excruciating slowness. I only catch bits of Nick's report on Levi's search efforts. A volunteer slipped, breaking his ankle, requiring another deputy to take him down the mountain and to the hospital. So only Levi and one other searcher must cover the entire search area.

Nick is assisting the Department of Wildlife in their search of Tweedy Mountain. My heart sinks at the thought of Sophie alone with Clive. While he showed no genuine interest in us, he'd been a less than generous caretaker. If food is scarce, it's a given that Sophie will get barely enough to keep her alive. If that. I refuse to consider the possibility Clive will cut his losses and run without Sophie. Would he leave her alone to die in the mountains or kill her himself?

"We're bringing Jess home tonight." Sly almost sings the words, and Maggie's grin stretches from ear to ear.

"So soon?" Uncle Mal sounds concerned.

"Yes," Sly responds. "After her fever broke, it never came back. She's been fever free for over forty-eight hours, so Dr. Kennedy said we could bring her home."

"She's pretty weak," Nick observes as he fills his plate with tonight's dinner, leftover chicken and noodles. "Maybe she can stay out of trouble." Sly uses her elbow to give him a friendly poke in the ribs. "Humph," he says, but his grin shows his relief too.

Cole enters the kitchen and smiles at Sly. "Ready?"

"Just waiting on you," Maggie teases, and Cole tugs on her single braid. The sound of their cheerful chatter follows them out the door.

Aunt Mary goes to Uncle Mal and leans into him. "But God," she whispers.

He bends down to kiss the top of her head, and I slip from the room, a sudden tightness in my throat. Only a few days ago, I'd stood with Cole as he shared his deepest fear of losing Jess. Now she's on her way home with what Dr. Kennedy claims is a genuine miracle. If only Sophie could have one of those too.

23

Jess

I scooch down in Dad's recliner, trying to find a comfortable position for my foot. The problem is once I arrange my foot, my back hurts. Even so, I'm happy to be home. After I limped down the stairs this morning, Sly shooed me into the living room and served me her delicious chocolate chip pancakes.

Maggie had flown through the room like a cyclone, eager to join her friends for a trip to the mall. "I'm late. Love you, Jess," had echoed behind her. I responded, but I'm sure she didn't hear me.

Sly comes into the room and hovers. I must be a little snappish. As she straightens the room, she calls me out. "I understand," she says. "You've been cooped up here since you got out of the hospital." She glances at her watch. "Almost eighteen hours ago."

I sense a bit of sarcasm, so I point out, "Not to mention five days in the hospital."

Her face softens. "How about I take you for a ride when I get back from the newspaper office this afternoon?" Sly hasn't been to work in almost a week and I'm sure she's eager to return. She's a reporter for the *Voice of Justice*. Her boss has been writing news stories about the bank robbery, but he is not the writer Sly is. Plus, she's eager to encourage more volunteers to join the search for Sophie.

I perk up at the thought of seeing the bustling streets of Justice. They must be more exciting than our living room. "Sounds good." My appreciation is genuine.

"Okay. Now, Grace will be here later, so please try to stay off your foot." Sly gathers up her laptop and turns to frown at me.

"What?" I ask. Maybe snappishly.

"I get that you're moving around well with that cane, but there's no need to take any chances. Dr. Kennedy said you'll be weak from the fever. There's no need to push it. You watch television until Grace stops by." I try to hide my grimace at Sly's words. I'm not a big fan of television. I'm a doer, not a watcher. And thinking of the make-up work I'll have elicits a sinking feeling in the pit of my stomach.

But I nod at Sly, and after another concerned frown, she leaves and I'm alone. I wish Cole had dropped off Roxie on his way to the stables this morning. Cole's shepherd and I have some great conversations about her owner. Despite all the sleep I've had, I doze off until I hear a car door slam outside. I glance at the clock and notice it's two-thirty in the afternoon. Too early for Grace.

I perk up when Sierra opens the door and pokes her head in. "Hey, are you up for a visitor?" she asks.

"Yes, please." I sit up straighter, eager for her company. Sierra glides into the room and, as usual, I feel a twinge of jealousy at her smooth movements. Sierra always seems to be poised, at least physically. She would never clomp or stumble the way I often do. Ugh. The bandage on my foot and the cane will make me even more clumsy.

"How are you?" Sierra lays a slender hand on my arm, and I smile.

"Better, now that you're here. Grace will join us in half an hour, and we can discuss the bank robbery." I notice a distinct lack of excitement in Sierra's gaze. "Or not."

Sierra shudders. "I'm not sure I'm up for that particular trip down memory lane." She settles into the sofa. "Is there anything I can get you?"

"Out of here."

"Can you leave?" She glances around as if she's looking for the Jess police.

"Of course. Sly was going to take me for a drive after work, but it would be nice to go out while the sun is still shining. By the time Sly gets home, it will be dark." I give Sierra a look Cole calls my "puppy dog eyes." I'm thankful Sierra is not as immune as Cole is.

"Well ... okay." she agrees uncertainly. "But I thought you said Grace is stopping by."

I consider the possibility of Grace making a fuss about me going out. If that happens, I guess I can have her call Sly at work. I squirm at the idea of needing my sister's permission to leave the house. I have a lot of people who love me, but sometimes there can be too many caretakers.

Surprisingly, after Grace arrives, she agrees. I pretend not to notice when she types a quick text, probably checking with Sly. Fine. Whatever. I don't care, I'm just happy to be free.

"Where would you like to go?" Sierra stops her car at the end of my driveway, waiting for my decision. She told me Nick had returned it that morning after they finished the forensics, checking it for clues. I can tell she's eager to be back on the road.

"I don't care, as long as I see mountains the entire way." My needs are simple.

"Mountains it is." Sierra turns right toward the Pioneer Mountains. We're silent for the first few minutes as Sierra and Grace let me soak up the beautiful scenery. Even in November, the mountains are breathtaking.

I catch Grace watching me from the corner of her eye as if I'm a bomb that's about to explode. I turn in frustration to tell her I'm fine, but a memory surfaces, stopping my words. Grace, sitting next to my bed in the hospital, praying. Crying. I'm riding in the backseat so I can keep my foot elevated on the seat. I reach forward and touch Grace's shoulder, and she turns to look at me.

"Jess? Are you okay?" Her blue eyes are wide with concern.

"I'm fine, Grace." I want to tell her she's a wonderful friend, and I love her. But the words catch in my throat. Grace, with her typical sensitivity, nods with a small smile. She reaches up to squeeze my hand that remains on her shoulder.

"Me too," she mouths, then turns to face forward.

As we near the intersection of I-15 and Route 238, Sierra asks, "Right or left?"

"Do you think we could go straight?" I ask. "I'd love to drive by Hadley's Ranch. It feels like years since I worked there."

"Sure," Sierra agrees. "Want to say hi to Cole?"

"No, that's okay. He's busy catching up on chores that he had to let go all week." I don't add that he'd probably have something to say about me being out and about already.

Sierra crosses the highway and follows the two-lane road that leads to Hadley's Ranch. As we pass the sprawling property, I'm disappointed none of the horses are in the corral. I especially miss Daisy. I like to think we bonded after our adventure in the woods facing the cougar, Outlaw.

A few miles down the road, a sign announces we are on the road to Bannack State Park.

"Should we go?" Sierra nods at the sign.

"Yes," I say.

"No," Grace says.

Doc Anderson's clinic is ahead on the right, and Sierra pulls into the parking lot. She turns off the engine and faces Grace and me. "Hey, I'm good either way," she says. "How much farther is it from here?"

"A million miles," Grace responds.

"May another ten or twelve," I say. I study the vet clinic where Cole and I raced to find treatment for Roxie after Outlaw attacked her in Bannack. I shiver as I remember that day.

Outlaw. Bannack. Something tugs at my mind, and I shake my head in frustration.

Grace turns from her whispered conversation with Sierra. "Jess, what's wrong? Does your foot hurt?" She reaches out to touch my face. "Your fever isn't back, is it?" The alarm in Grace's voice breaks my concentration and I hurry to reassure her.

"No, I'm good. I had a weird feeling I should remember something." My voice trails off as I try to focus. *Outlaw. Bannack. Sophie.* Wait! My dream. I sit up straighter. "Um, guys, we need to go to Bannack."

Grace eyes me suspiciously. "Why?"

I swallow and try to make my voice sound reasonable and sure. "I think Sophie is there."

24

Jess

"This is a terrible idea." Grace peers through the blowing snow. Of course, the snow started about five minutes after we left the clinic.

Sierra leans forward and squints through the windshield. "At least it's not coming down heavy, it's just blowing."

"Well, blowing snow makes the roads slippery, so, yeah, terrible idea." Grace reaches for the grab bar, and her fingers tighten until they turn white. "We should have waited for Nick and the team to meet us at the clinic."

"We don't know when they'll receive our message. In the meantime, Sophie is living through a nightmare. We need to find her as soon as we can," I say.

"You should try to call Nick or Cole again." Sierra's voice is tight with stress. The sun is setting, and soon she'll need her headlights to travel the twisting mountain road.

"No, the cell service is terrible the higher we go up the mountain. I sent Nick and Cole texts, telling them where we are heading. I'm sure they're on their way right now."

Sierra glances at Grace. "Grab my phone out of my purse? I have good reception, even in the mountains."

Grace rummages through Sierra's purse and pulls out the phone. "Wow, it's still got three bars."

I lean forward. "Sierra, why don't you call Levi?"

Her sudden burst of laughter startles me.

"Oh sure, I'll simply call him up and say, 'Hi Levi. Jess, Grace, and I are driving up a snowy mountain road to a ghost town to confront a kidnapper with a gun. Have a nice night.'" Sierra shudders at the thought.

I frown, imagining my own upcoming conversations.

"I'll call him," Grace offers.

Sierra sighs but supplies the unlock code, and soon Grace is scrolling through her contacts. "*Hmm*, it is interesting that Levi is listed in your phone as Dashing Deputy Levi." Grace's tone is teasing, and the mood in the car lightens as Grace texts Levi.

Sierra shrugs. "Not on me. Levi put his number in my phone."

"Curiouser and curiouser," I tease.

From my spot in the backseat, I notice a faint flush rise in Sierra's cheek. She clears her throat. "Let's focus on rescuing Sophie."

Grace shifts in her seat and says, "Jess, tell us the dream again."

I sigh. "I was in Bannack, being chased by Outlaw."

"The cougar?" Sierra confirms.

"Yes."

"And when did you see Sophie?" Grace asks.

"I saw her when I ran out from behind the schoolhouse onto the main street. She was standing in the middle of the parking lot."

"Alone?" Sierra asks.

"Alone."

"Well, I can understand why you might dream about Outlaw and Bannack, based on your experience. And it even makes sense why Sophie was in your dream. But how did you come up with Sophie being in Bannack?" Sierra's tone is gentle.

"Leopard Woman and Rochelle," I explain. "When we started talking about Bannack and Outlaw, I remembered something I overheard the first day I saw those two women."

"At Verity's?" Grace asks.

"Yep. Remember, Grace, when they first went to Verity's register, they were asking her about things to do in Dillon. Susie —er—Rochelle said something about Bannack, asking if it was closed for the season. Verity said it was. Tourists always ask questions about Bannack, so I didn't think about it. It came back to me a few minutes ago, their conversation about Bannack and the dream. I think there's a good chance Sophie is being held there."

"I'm not sure about how dreams work," Sierra says. "Do you think a cougar is waiting for us too?"

"No," I answer with certainty. "In the dream, I kept saying, 'The Outlaw is in Bannack.' I think in this dream, Clive is the outlaw."

THE SNOW IS GETTING HEAVIER by the time we reach Bannack. Never in my wildest dreams would I have imagined this is where I'd spend my evening. I'm certain it's not what Sly had in mind, either. Poor Sly. I need to be a better sister. A calmer sister. I'll get right on that tomorrow.

Sierra stops the car at the end of the parking lot and turns off the engine. I approve of the spot where she's placed us. The Bannack sign is on one side, and a row of trees hides us on the other side. "We'll need to walk in from here," she says, reaching into the glove box for a flashlight.

I gaze at the old buildings of Bannack. During nine months of the year, the abandoned town is a tourist attraction for anyone who wants to visit the Gold Rush days. But now the shuttered buildings hold no charm. We walk in a route close to the tree line, so we won't be visible if Clive is watching. The twilight offers enough illumination for us to find our way. My cane leaves perfect circles in the snow as we move.

"I've visited Bannack so many times in my life, I've memorized it by heart," I say. "I believe the visitor's center is the only building that has electricity and water. If the caretakers left that on through the winter, it would make sense for Clive to keep Sophie there."

I glance down at my previously white cast and grimace at the soggy mess.

Sierra whispers, "Is this your first time back since, well ... you know?"

I stumble a little, and Grace moves to my side, steadying me. "You mean since a huge mountain lion tried to kill me and the people I love?" I give a brisk nod.

"At least we won't have to battle the wildlife this time," Grace whispers. We creep around behind the schoolhouse, and Grace and I exchange glances. The memory of our terror is still fresh. As we near the back of the visitor's center, there's a whirring sound coming from the generator powering the electricity. At least if Sophie is here, she isn't cold.

My heart sinks when I discover the double lock on the back door. "Guys, I don't think we'll be able to get through this way. Let's go around to the front and check what that lock is like." We edge along the side of the building, trying to stay in the shadows. I lead the posse up the wooden steps and across the wide plank porch in front of the building.

As I study the lock, I suggest, "Grace, can you go around to the other side to find out if there is another door or a window?" Grace sidles past me and disappears into the darkness.

Sierra and I nearly knock heads as we both lean in to examine the door lock. "At least there's no deadbolt on this one." Sierra steps back. "We could try to pick the lock with a hairpin or something." Her eyes dart around as if expecting hairpins to be falling from the sky like snow.

I reach up to pull a bobby pin from my hair. Fortunately, Maggie wanted to learn French braiding, and last night she used my head for practice. My hair is full of the bobby pins she used to hold my rioting curls in place.

Sierra leans closer to the shop window and cups her hands around her eyes, trying to peek inside. "There's a flickering light in the back," she whispers. "A candle or a kerosene lamp?" I try to finesse the pin into the lock, but it breaks. Oh well, I've got plenty. I reach up and pull another one from my braid.

Grace appears at my side, breathing hard in the cold air. "I saw Sophie," she pants. "She's in a storage room or office. I couldn't tell. There's a window, and I could see her lying on a cot."

Sierra pushes past me to go around the building, but Grace lays a hand on her arm. "I tried knocking on the window, but she didn't move."

"She's alive though, right?" Sierra's voice rises in fear.

"Yes, I could see her breathing, but she didn't respond to the noise. I think Clive drugged her."

Sierra's hiss is furious. "He is such a coward if he's so afraid of a twelve-year-old girl that he has to drug her."

Anger radiates off Sierra, and I feel my temper boil too. It's time to put an end to Clive's reign of terror. I turn back to my lock-picking project while Sierra and Grace inspect the window for any weakness.

"Look." Grace points. "I think there's a cat in there." She and Sierra put their noses up to the window. I'm so focused on listening to their conversation that I almost miss the sound—a slight click. I think I've released the lock.

My hope is shattered as something hard presses into my side and I realize the click was Clive cocking the pistol that is digging into my liver.

"Um, guys." My throat is dry, and the words come out scratchy. Sierra and Grace continue to focus on the cat inside the store, discussing whether they can lure it to help us.

"Doubtful." Grace sounds disappointed, and I suspect she's imagining possible cat heroics.

"Grace." I make the word sharp, and she jerks her head in surprise at my tone. In the dim light of the moon, I can see her face pale, making her freckles luminescent. Grace uses her elbow to nudge Sierra, who grunts and turns to face us. Sierra's eyes narrow the second she spots Clive. I long to step back to be out of range of the laser focus of her rage.

"You." Clive snarls, and to my horror, Sierra takes a step forward, looking like an avenging angel. Grace grabs her arm and pulls her back.

"I'm done with you," Clive growls. "Stand right there, or I'll give your friend here another bullet to match the one Rochelle gave her. Only it won't be in her foot."

Sweat trickles down my neck, although the temperature must be in the twenties. Nausea roils up in my stomach, and I do my best not to throw up.

Clive lifts his booted foot and administers a hearty kick to the door, yelling, "Maude, get out here!" Grace and Sierra's eyes mirror my confusion. Maude? Where does Clive come up with these women willing to help him commit felonies? The door swings open, and a middle-aged woman stares at me, Grace, and Sierra, then turns to Clive.

"Uh-uh, no way. One hostage is my limit. What do I look like, a den mother?" She stomps away into the gift shop, and Clive motions for us to follow her. Shaking, we step inside. The cat leaps down from the table, where he has been staying warm near the kerosene lamp.

"What did I tell you about that cat?" Clive kicks the door shut without removing the gun from my side. I assume I'll have a round bruise there tomorrow.

If I have a tomorrow.

25

Jess

"I t's either the cat or the lamp, Maude. You can't have 'em both. Too dangerous." Clive removes the gun from my ribs and waves it toward a closed door near the back of the room.

"That way," he orders, and we reluctantly move. "Maude, grab the key and open the door."

Maude does it, mumbling under her breath. "How you think you're gonna keep these chickees alive?" The door swings open to show an office and storage room barely illuminated by a kerosene lamp.

"Inside." Clive snarls, motioning Sierra and Grace inside. He reaches for my cane and tosses it into the hallway, then shoulders me inside the room too. Sierra hurries to the cot where Sophie is sleeping. At least, I hope she's just asleep. "Isn't that precious," Clive sneers. Then he slams the door behind us. A moment later an argument begins.

"I'm tellin' you, Clive, I ain't takin' care of no more girls. I told Ma your plan wouldn't work, but she said, 'Now, Maudie, your brother is the smartest one in our family. If he says he's got a way to get us some actual cash, then he's gonna do it.'"

I press my ear against the door to hear the plan. Their voices fade as they move away, but they're still arguing.

"You've always been Ma's favorite, being the baby and all," Maude continues. "I'm gonna call her and tell her what is going on. You're mixed up with the cartels now, and that's a death sentence for sure."

Clive's voice is quieter but still threatening. "You're not calling anyone."

"Whatcha doing with that gun, Clive? You gonna shoot your sister now?" Maude taunts him, and I have a wave of concern. I don't want to be Maude's best friend, but I don't want her to be dead, either.

"Stop hammering at me and let me think." Clive's words trail off as they seem to move farther away. I hold my breath, waiting for a gunshot.

Nothing. I finally relax. Maude might live another day.

I join Grace on a blanket she's spread on the floor next to Sophie's cot. Sierra sits beside Sophie, smoothing the girl's hair away from her face. "I can't wake her up," Sierra sobs. "I'm not sure what they gave her."

"Well, she's breathing okay," Grace points out. "Let's keep trying to wake her so she'll be ready to go with us when we escape."

"We're escaping?" Sierra and I speak at the same time.

"Of course," Grace says with confidence. "This kind of reminds me of the lesson I taught in Sunday School class last week. When guards locked Paul and Silas in jail, they sang worship songs, and God sent an earthquake to help them escape."

Sierra and I stare at her.

"What? It's in the Bible."

"Yes," I draw out the word. "But let's ask God to save the earthquake as a last resort."

"I didn't have an earthquake on my Bingo card for today," Sierra mutters as she shakes Sophie.

"So, what did you overhear when you were listening to Maude and Clive?" Grace appears to have recovered from our rejection of the earthquake option. I repeat the conversation as best I can and notice a frown forming between Grace's eyebrows.

"What is it?" I ask.

"I guess I never thought of Clive having a mother," Grace says.

Sierra surprises me with her giggle. "Or that Maude would tattle to her about little brother Clive's mess-up."

I snicker, picturing that conversation. Then I return my focus to the reality of our situation. We have to get out of here. Whatever Clive has planned for us, it's not good. I prowl the room, looking for a tool to use to help us escape. The window is our best option, so we don't chance running into Clive and Maude.

I pick up a broom and tap the handle against the window, hoping I can shatter the glass. Quietly. That will be the challenge.

"It won't work."

I turn. Sophie is rubbing her eyes, as Sierra hugs her.

"I tried it before." Sophie is groggy but begins to shake off the effects of whatever drug Clive gave her.

Sierra takes Sophie's face in her hands. "Sophie, did Clive hurt you at all?"

Sophie frowns. "No, I haven't seen Clive since the day he brought me here after he took me off the mountain. He left me with Maude and said he was going to search for Travis before the cartel killed them all." Sophie shudders and Sierra wraps the blanket tighter around her.

"Okay." Sierra takes a deep breath and repeats, "Okay."

"Maybe if we all hold the broom and swing the handle at the window, we can break it." Grace takes the broom from me and hefts it in her hands.

Sophie shakes her head and points to the corner, where two brooms lie, shattered in pieces. "It's not strong enough against the reinforced glass. I saved that last one for a weapon. Maude got tired of me pounding on the door, so yesterday she put something in my food." Sophie glances around the room. "Is there any water in there?" She nods at a metal pitcher sitting on the desk.

Sierra hurries to check but shakes her head. "I'm sorry, it's empty."

"You poor thing," Grace pulls a water bottle out from the zippered pocket of her jacket. "Here you go, honey." At Sierra's raised eyebrow, Grace says, "What? I was in Awana when I lived in Georgia. We did a lesson on basic survival skills. I always carry a water bottle."

"It's true," I confirm. "Of course, she also knows where every rest stop is between here and Missoula, but at least she's always hydrated."

Sophie sips the water gratefully and returns the bottle to Grace. "We need to save some in case Maude forgets us."

The word 'again' is unspoken. Just how long has Sophie gone without water during her captivity? We're quiet for a few minutes, lost in our own thoughts.

Sophie breaks the silence with a question. "Are you two Jess and Grace?"

"Yes." Grace and I answer together.

"Thought so. Sierra told me stories about some of the stuff you've done." Sophie's grin is small but genuine. "It figures you two would show up here." There's an element of hope in her voice, and I sincerely pray we don't disappoint her.

"I think Grace was on to something, earlier," Sierra says. "I mean, think about it. Paul and Silas didn't expect God to cause an earthquake. They just sang worship songs."

"True," Grace agrees. "I've been sitting here thinking about one of my favorite songs. It's from Psalm 32:7 Let's start with that one." Grace sings, "You are my hiding place."

"Perfect," Sierra agrees and joins in. I hesitate. Singing is not my gift. But as the encouraging words surround me, I soon join the song. Glancing over at Sophie, I notice her eyes are closed and she isn't singing. I stumble over the words, realizing Sophie may not know the song.

Sierra takes Sophie's hand in her own, and I watch as silent tears trickle down Sophie's cheeks. Peace settles over her face, and I smile, turning away to join in the singing. Hard pounding on the door interrupts us. I grab the broom by the bristle end, ready to swing it at the first head that pokes through the door.

"Shut up in there," Clive yells.

"Make us!" My mouth falls open at Grace's words. She's almost as shocked as I am.

I give her my best what-are-you-thinking look, and she shrugs, moving closer.

"He has to open the door so you can hit him on the head," she explains.

I shake my head but tighten my grip on the broom.

"What did you say, little girl?" Clive is fired up now.

"She said you're a coward and a bully." Sierra joins us, pulling Sophie along with her. "Be ready to run as soon as Jess knocks him out," she whispers to Sophie. How did my idea of hitting Clive with the broom morph from my instinct into their plan?

The key turns in the lock, and we all four draw in a synchronized breath as Clive pushes open the door. The next minutes seem to play out in slow motion. Clive steps into the room, and I swing the broom.

There's a solid *thwack*, then I drop the broom as the impact vibrates almost up to my elbows. I misjudged his height. Rather than his head, the broom handle connects with his arm.

Sierra shouts, "Sophie, run!" as Clive faces me. I flash mentally to a documentary about grizzly bears, and I'm stunned by Clive's resemblance to the animal. I step back, then several things happen at once.

From the reception area, Maude yells, "Clive!"

Something heavy clatters to the floor, and the cat emits a furious meow. There's the sound of shattering glass and a soft *whoosh*. What could that be?

I don't have time to think about it as Clive stalks me. He reaches for his gun, then lowers his gaze to the floor, his grin evil. "Ah, yeah, this will teach ya," he sneers.

Before I have time to register his words, he lifts his booted foot and stomps down on my soft cast.

As my vision hazes, turning to black, I have one thought. *What's whooshing?*

26

Saturday
November 23
5:00 p.m.

Sierra

I push and half carry Sophie through the doorway and into the larger room, where Maude sits stroking her cat. When she spots us she yells, "Clive," and drops the cat, who hisses and leaps for the table. Horrified, I watch as the cat swings around in fury, catching the edge of the kerosene lamp that is the only source of light in the room.

Maude races towards Sophie and me and grabs my sleeve. I turn and give Maude a solid push, and she stumbles back. I jump as the cat flies through the air, making a noise I've never heard come from a cat. Maude and I turn to watch the flame from the lamp soak up the spilled kerosene and race across the wooden floor.

I should grab Sophie and run, but I'm momentarily mesmerized by the flames as they climb up a tall rack filled with travel pamphlets describing the tourist attractions of Montana.

In seconds, the fire consumes the brochures, leaving wisps of scorched paper to float in the air like burning snowflakes.

Maude gasps then screams, "Clive! Fire!"

I grab Sophie's arm and pull her to the door, yank it open, and hurl us into the cold air and snow. We turn to gape as flames devour the wooden rafters near the ceiling. "Where are Jess and Grace?" Sophie gasps.

"They must still be inside. I didn't see anything after Jess hit Clive. You stay here. I'm going to go find them."

"No!" Sophie steps in front of me. "We'll both go. One of us can distract Clive, and the other can get Jess and Grace out before the fire gets to the storage room."

I open my mouth to protest, but Sophie shakes my arm and points toward the building. Inside, I watch Clive stagger over to Maude, and tug her toward the front door. Toward us. Clive bellows when he spots us, and I assume they can hear him back in Justice. He takes a menacing step in our direction as the cat launches itself through the open door.

Maude screeches, "Cally, come back here," and then she stumbles through the door after her pet. Clive reaches into his pocket and pulls out his gun. I grab Sophie's arm and run along the building, dragging her after me. We both slip as we run in the snow.

"Here." I pull Sophie around the corner of the building, trying to think of a place where I can hide her. It's been several years since my mom and I visited Bannack. Between the growing fire and the mini blizzard, I'm disoriented.

Clive's boots crunch in the snow as he stalks us, and we're forced to move farther away from the burning building. Farther away from any chance of rescuing Jess and Grace. Tears of fear and fury sting my eyes.

"Let's circle back to get them." Sophie's whisper is vaguely discernable as the wind howls around us. I want to say no, but reconsider. Clive won't expect that. He thinks we're running away from him, running for our lives. Well, he's not wrong. But he doesn't understand the concepts of love and loyalty. I nod, and we retrace our steps.

In the distance, Maude calls, "Cally! Calico Cat, where are you?" We slip behind the building next door to the visitors' center. My heart stutters when Clive's voice sounds way too close.

"C'mon out now. I promise I won't hurt ya'. We need to talk about this." His wheedling is even more annoying than his threats. We stop and I hold my breath, waiting for Clive to speak again and give us his location. For a criminal, he's kind of stupid. Long seconds pass, and my heart aches at the thought of Jess and Grace trapped in the fire.

It's almost as if Clive reads my mind because his next words shatter my heart. "Your friends are dead. Burned up in the fire." He snarls the words. "I saw it myself."

27

Saturday
November 23
5:30 p.m.

Jess

I wake up as someone slaps my cheeks. Hard. "Ouch." I open my eyes to see Grace's tear-streaked face.

"We have to break out of here." Grace jumps up from the floor where I'm lying, and I try to remember how I got there.

The room is uncomfortably warm, and the smell of noxious smoke chokes me. My throbbing foot brings the memory back into detail. "I think I'm going to be sick."

"No time," Grace says, not unsympathetically. "Escape the fire. After that, you can puke." I'm momentarily distracted by Grace's use of the word *puke*. She hates that word. Wait. What else did she say? Fire.

"Fire?" I lift myself up on my elbows. There's definitely smoke in the air. "Where?"

Grace points to the closed door. "Out there."

"Where are Sierra and Sophie?" I groan as Grace helps me

133

stand up. My foot is throbbing, and I nearly collapse again, but Grace is stronger than she appears.

"I think they got out." Grace positions my arm across her shoulder. "At least, I pray they got out."

I lose the fight to stop my tears. "Please, God," I whisper.

We stagger to the door, and Grace peeks out into the main room. She jerks her head back and shuts the door. "We can't go out that way. The fire is blocking the exit." We both turn to glare at the window, which had resisted our escape attempts earlier.

I contemplate the room. "Where's the broom?"

Grace flushes. "Um, I broke it over Clive's head. When I saw him stomp on your injured foot, I was so angry ..." her voice trails off, and I reach over to give her a tight hug.

"It didn't slow him down much. Maude yelled, 'Fire!' and he ran out the door, locking us in." The defeat in her voice breaks my heart. Usually, Grace is the encourager.

"Grace, look at me."

She peers up, and even through the dim light she instantly reads the truth in my eyes. Hope. We say the words in unison, and it feels good. "But God."

I try to focus as the throbbing in my foot increases. "Maybe we missed something. Let's check those shelves for anything we can use to pry the window up." I hobble to the tallest metal shelf and rummage around, pushing aside toilet paper, cleaning spray, and vacuum bags. Grace is frantically searching the other shelf, but she has to stop at times due to her coughing.

I'm aware of the smoke seeping under the door, but I push down panic. Inspiration hits as I find a jumbo roll of paper towels. and tear a long strip. Next, I reach for the plastic water bottle and soak the towel. I fold it in half and hand it to Grace. "Here, hold this over your mouth to keep the smoke out."

Grace takes the wet towel. "You, too."

"Of course." I repeat the process and resume my search. The sound of the fire consuming the outer room is becoming louder.

My heart races, and a pool of fear forms in the pit of my stomach.

Beside me, Grace whispers, "But God." A thought tickles my mind, and despite our circumstances, I smile.

"Hey, Grace?"

"Yes?"

"Maybe you should have told your Sunday school class the story of Shadrach, Meshack, and Abednego in the fiery furnace. Jesus was in the fire with them."

Grace's eyes widen above the soggy paper towels. "Actually, that's next week's Bible story."

AFTER WHAT FEELS LIKE AN ETERNITY, I sit on the cot next to Grace.

We've searched every square inch of this room and there is nothing we can use to break the window. We tried to pry out the broken lock, but it wouldn't budge. The knowledge that freedom and safety are on the other side is devastating.

We stopped searching and now sit on the floor trying to conserve as much oxygen as possible. Above us, the smoke is getting thicker, and Grace is coughing almost constantly. She had pneumonia this past summer, and although she recovered, the doctor gave her an inhaler to use for a few months until her lungs were stronger. But she rarely carries it these days.

I study my best friend. Her strawberry blonde hair is limp with sweat, and tear streaks make winding paths through the freckles on her cheeks. "You could've escaped." I make it a statement and not a question.

Grace's expression doesn't change, but I sense a new alertness in her.

"You were behind Sierra and Sophie as they ran. They thought we were all escaping. But you came back." Grace doesn't respond, so I continue. My throat hurts, and my voice is raspy.

"Even when Maude yelled 'fire,' the door was still open. You could have run out at that point. But you stayed."

"You were unconscious. You couldn't run away."

Like that answers the question. Maybe it does. Sometimes love is that simple.

I reach for her hand and whisper, "Thank you."

She laces her fingers through mine and smiles. The heat in the room is becoming unbearable, and smoke fills the air. My eyes water, and tears stream unchecked down my face.

Grace asks, "Do you think we're going to die in here?" I'm not surprised by her words, since she just spoke my thoughts. Before I answer, she continues, "What do you think heaven is like?"

I've given this a lot of thought since Mamma and Daddy died. "Well, I don't think we'll be sitting on clouds playing the harp for all of eternity."

"Me either," Grace agrees. "When you think about how beautiful and amazing this world is, I think heaven will be a million times better. It will be breathtaking and fascinating and full of adventure."

"And Jesus," Grace adds.

"And love," I say. Then I close my eyes.

28

Sierra

Beside me, Sophie sobs quietly. I grip her hand and squeeze, my throat too tight to speak. Clive's lying. Jess and Grace can't be dead! I move toward the visitor center, trying to ignore the choking smoke that hangs like a cloud around us. We dart along the burning building and discover the window to the storage room. The moon has slipped behind some clouds, so it's difficult to see inside.

The front part of the building is engulfed in flame, but this back corner is still intact. I touch the window to check for heat and I'm surprised to find it cold. I brush aside the snow clinging to the pane and turn on my flashlight, careful not to let it shine toward the main street, where Clive and Maude are arguing. Their muffled words drift away, and I hope they are far enough down the street that they won't notice my light.

The flashlight illuminates the edge of the shelf holding

cleaning supplies. Beside me, Sophie edges closer, whispering, "What do you see? Are they in there?" A sudden tap from the inside of the window causes us to jump back in alarm. I stifle my startled scream. Sophie lets out a yip. We wait in silence, terrified Clive has heard her.

The tapping on the window draws me back, and I shine my light into the room again. Two pairs of eyes appear out of the dark, and I jump back, dropping the flashlight. Sophie grabs it and holds it steady for me as I cup my hands around my eyes, peering through the window. Jess and Grace huddle together on the other side.

"They're alive." Beside me, Sophie emits a happy gasp that ends in a tiny sob. "We have to break the window." I look around for something to use. I consider hitting the window with the end of my flashlight. But the end is made of rubber, so I discard that idea.

Tapping turns to pounding as Jess and Grace frantically try to break the window with the end of a broken broom. I could use the flashlight to send them a message with Morse code. That's a great idea. I sure wish I knew Morse code. Of course, they probably don't know it either. Sophie is no longer beside me and I turn in circles, trying to spot her.

"Sophie," I hiss.

She materializes with a report. "Clive and Maude are walking toward their car. I bet they're afraid someone saw the fire and called the fire department. I think they're leaving."

I'm relieved, but furious at the thought of them escaping.

"The fire is spreading fast," Sophie continues her report. "There's no way to open the front door. This window is our only hope."

"You stay here and try to keep them calm. I'm going to grab the tire iron from my trunk. I think it can break the window." Sophie nods, and I hurry to the front of the building, relieved to see the taillights of Clive's car heading down the mountain.

I race across the snow-covered ground, only slipping once

before I reach my car and click the lock for the trunk. As it swings up, I remember putting the tire iron back here after my recent flat tire. Pushing aside sneakers, flip-flops, a sweater, blanket, and a half-full bag of Cheetos, I grimace. Ick. I find a bag of paper trash from the last time I "cleaned out" the car.

Sophie has the flashlight, and as I reach farther back into the trunk, I lose any help from the moonlight. Finally, my fingers touch something hard, and I pull out the tire iron. Seconds later, I'm racing across the parking lot. As I near the visitors' center, I'm shocked by the power of the fire. It has engulfed the entire left side of the building, and I shudder, as part of the roof falls into the flames.

I think of Jess and Grace trapped in that small storage room as fear pools in my stomach. We only have a few minutes to rescue them. I slide into Sophie and nearly knock her over. "Stand over there, away from the window," I say.

"Jess! Grace!" I pound on the window and their shadowy faces appear. "Take the blanket off the cot and hold it in front of the window." I try to ignore the orange glow of the fire as it flickers behind the door. My heart pounds to the rhythm of the words *hurry, hurry, hurry* roaring in my mind. I wave the tire iron so they can see. "The blanket will shield you." Again, I point at the cot and wave my weapon.

It takes far too long to get my meaning across, but when the window breaks, I don't want to cut them. Finally, one of them goes to grab the blanket and a second later, the lower half of the window is black as they raise the blanket.

Coughing from inside the room urges me forward. I hold the tire iron horizontally, and, using the pronged end, drive it into the lower edge of the window.

Nothing happens.

I pull it back, and applying as much force as I can, I ram the end into the window again. And again. And again.

The coughing increases. My face warms then instantly chills as the wind catches the tears streaming down my cheeks. *Please,*

God. I continue to hammer away, but nothing happens. Just as my arms start to give way, I hear a new sound. Jess and Grace are singing a worship song. I catch the melody and join them.

"You are my hiding place." I turn into a baseball hitter's stance and swing the tire iron with all of my strength.

Crack!

I don't check, I just keep swinging.

29

Jess

"D'you hear that?" Grace stands and moves toward the window.

"Clive?"

"Clive wouldn't try to reach us through the window. He would simply let the fire do the job for him." Grace puts her nose right up to the window, then yelps when a beam of light shines in her eyes.

I squint until I make out the shadowy outlines of two people. Sierra and Sophie! Grace and I tap on the window to catch their attention. Soon our tapping turns to pounding. A few minutes pass, but it feels like forever.

Behind me, the wooden door cracks as the fire rages against it. We only have a few minutes before the door collapses and the little oxygen that's left in here will suck the fire right in.

When Sierra instructs us to use the blanket to protect us

from the broken glass, I'm staggered by hope. I fumble in the acrid darkness and find the blanket. Grace and I feel the edges of the window frame and hold up the blanket. The first thud of the tire iron against the window is heartbreaking. Not even the tiniest crack. We can't see what's happening, but the thuds increase to no effect.

In my heart, I cry out, *Jesus, be in the fire with us!*

I focus on the window while my heart thunders in rhythm to the strikes. Praying. Even just a flicker of hope would be welcome. What was that? I stare harder. Did I hear something or is my mind playing tricks?

Crack!

It's the most beautiful sound in the world.

Sierra continues to batter the window, and soon shards of glass are dropping onto the floor. I glance behind me as the fire crackles. If the door breaks before the window, the fire will race toward us.

Oxygen fuels fire, and this fire is coming for what's left of the air in the room. Now more air will enter through the broken window.

My throat burns. I don't have the breath to speak the words, but my heart continues to beat to the rhythm of *hurry, hurry, hurry*."

Moments later, the bulk of the glass shatters and falls into the blanket. Grace and I use the blanket to sweep the glass to the floor, then see Sierra and Sophie standing on the other side. They clear the glass from their side so we can climb through.

"Careful," Sierra cautions. "More glass will fall, so keep your head down."

She reaches through the window, and I shove the blanket over the edge where the panes were. As she grasps my arm, I notice the bracelet Cole gave me for my birthday just a few weeks ago. The word *Brave* is engraved on the leather cuff, and I'm thankful for the reminder.

Taking a deep breath of the cold air, I stand on my tiptoes, trying to hoist myself to the windowsill. I balance there for only a second. Then I begin to slide back into the storage room. No. This can't be happening. We are so close to freedom.

All of a sudden, Grace wraps her arms around my legs and boosts me up and through the window. I land inelegantly at Sierra's feet and scramble up. We must get Grace out too. But Grace is shorter than I am. And there's no one there to lift her as she did for me.

"Give me your arm." Sierra's voice is frantic as she reaches to grab Grace's elbow. Shoving my hand through the opening, I grab her other elbow. The office door gives a last crack, allowing the fire to swarm into the room with a greedy roar.

Sierra and I pull together, but Grace barely budges off the floor. Nausea swirls as my foot throbs, leeching away my strength. The open window is feeding the fire, which is now only a few feet from Grace.

Sierra and I pull again.

Grace's face contorts into a puzzled frown just before she sails through the window, knocking us all down.

"Run!" Sierra grabs Sophie's hand. Grace clambers to her feet and stabilizes me as we hobble to the front of the building. Behind us, the fire whooshes through the open window. Seconds. That was all the time we'd had.

But God.

30

*Saturday
November 23
6:00 p.m.*

Jess

G race and Sierra help me limp to the car. The adrenaline is fading, and the pain in my foot increases. By the time they lean me against the fender of the car, tears are falling. Behind us, the fire roars and snaps as the building is fully engulfed, and light flares up, illuminating the parking lot.

I begin to shake and recognize the signs of shock. Earlier I'd refused to acknowledge my weakness, which is a consequence of my fever from the infection. Now I focus every bit of strength I have on remaining upright.

"We need to put her in the backseat and prop up her foot." Grace reaches for my arm again, but I shake my head. I regret my mistake as the trees, buildings, and my friends swirl before my eyes. I shut them tight, but the vertigo is overwhelming.

"Not yet." It takes every ounce of strength I have to whisper the words.

Grace and Sierra appear worried as I open my eyes. I want to reassure them, tell them I'll be fine, but I'm pretty sure that would be a lie. My eyes close again. Voices and movement surround me, but I can only concentrate on not sliding down the side of the car, into the drifting snow.

A car door slams, and I'm puzzled. Sierra sent Sophie to open the back door of the car to drag me in. Opening the door doesn't make that sound.

There's more slamming, but it doesn't matter, it's too far away. Grace and Sierra move, and my body betrays me. I slither down the bumper.

"Here, I'll take her." Strong arms lift me, and I snuggle into the warmth of a rough flannel jacket. Has a lumberjack rescued me?

A familiar scent tickles my nose as I smile. Piney aftershave.

Cole.

I open my eyes. Nick and Levi hurry ahead to open the back door of Nick's SUV. Cole crawls backward into the vehicle, holding me tightly as Nick protects my injured foot.

The once white bandage is now red. Blood. I close my eyes again and lean against Cole's chest. Nick elevates my foot on the seat, then closes the door and I'm alone with Cole.

"Hi," I say, groggily.

He doesn't respond at first, but I'm aware of the tension in his body.

Finally, he says, "Hi yourself." The words are right, but the tone is off. He's scared or mad. Again. Poor Cole, I think as I drift off. I'm a very high-maintenance girlfriend.

31

Saturday
November 23
6:05 p.m.

Sierra

A hand tugs on my arm and I swing around, face-to-face with a concerned Levi. His brow furrows as he glances up and down, gauging my status.

"Are you hurt?" His words are abrupt.

"No." I step away from his hold and raise my chin a bit. "No, I'm fine."

He watches me for a moment and nods sharply. "Good," he says and walks away. Well, okay then.

I search for Sophie and pull her into a hug. "It's all over now," I reassure her. "It's time to go home." At her stark expression, I remember the conversations we've had in the weeks that I've been her mentor. Home is not a happy place for Sophie. My throat tightens, but all I can say is, "It's going to be okay, Sophie. I promise."

The lightening of her expression stabs my heart. How can I

promise her that? I'm not a social worker. I have no authority to change her living situation. But Uncle Malcolm can help. He has to.

I hear Nick talking into his department-issued radio. "Repeat, missing girl Sophie Granger is found." The dispatcher says something, but I can't decipher the crackly voice. "Roger that," Nick says. "Firefighting units on the way."

I'm sure he's afraid the other buildings, old and dry as tinder, will catch. I look around, relieved that so far that doesn't seem to have happened.

Nick approaches and studies Sophie and me. "All good?" he asks, and we both nod. "Sierra, give your keys to Levi. He's going to drive you and Sophie back to town. Grace, Cole, and Jess are with me."

I want to protest that I'm fine to drive, but Levi is standing beside Nick and gives a slight shake of his head. My hands tremble, and I relent. Silently, I hand Levi the keys and climb into the backseat of my car with Sophie.

"Why don't you sit in the front?" she suggests. "I'd kind of like to lie down back here if that's okay." I nibble the inside of my lip in indecision. I'm not sure I want to ride next to Levi. But Sophie is almost asleep on her feet, so I agree.

"Buckle the lap belt around you."

"Yes, Mom." Sophie surprises me with a genuine smile, and I give her a quick hug. I settle into the front passenger seat, and a moment later Levi is beside me, starting the engine. We follow Nick's squad car down the mountain, and I keep my eyes trained on the road.

Will we catch up with Clive and Maude? I need to focus on the positive, but the thought of them escaping arrest makes me angry. We found Sophie, and we're all alive. That's a win.

Less than a mile down the road, I hear sirens. A ladder fire truck and two tankers rush past us, toward Bannack. Nick pauses at the approach of an SUV, and Levi comes to a halt behind him.

"That's the fire chief's car," Levi says, lowering his window.

Nick gives the chief a quick report, then his squad car moves on and we roll along behind it.

"Why did you go up the mountain?" Levi's words startle me, and I turn to face him. I try to remain calm as I describe Jess's dream and her memory of Leopard Woman and Rochelle asking Verity about Bannack.

"It seemed likely Clive was hiding Sophie up there, and we needed to go check."

He sends me a look I interpret as, "That was stupid."

"We called you and Nick on the way." I defend myself.

"Why didn't you pull off and wait for us?"

I've been expecting this question. "We were worried Clive might move again. It was too risky." I sit back, satisfied with my logic.

"How many roads go up to Bannack?" Levi asks, and I'm caught off guard.

"Um, I'm not sure. How many?" I answer his question with my own.

"Guess," he insists.

I see where he's going with this. "One?"

"One. If Clive left Bannack, you would have seen him on Bannack Road, right? You could have described his vehicle and even given the license plate. You and Jess and Grace would have been safe in the car while Nick and I caught Clive and saved Sophie. Correct?" He glances at me like he expects an answer.

I shrug. "Maybe," I concede.

"Maybe safe is better than not safe at all," Levi snaps, and I turn away to gaze out the front window. Before I can respond, Levi says, "I'm disappointed in you."

My mouth falls open in shock and hurt. I want to reply, but he's on a roll.

"You were the adult in the car, Sierra. As mature as Grace and Jess are, they are seventeen years old. You are almost twenty. You were the driver and had the right to say, 'No, I won't risk our lives by confronting a kidnapper. I won't transport us to an abandoned town where we will be in danger from a fire.'" Levi's voice is getting louder with each word, and my throat is tight with unshed tears. Levi is right. I hate that.

"She did it for me." Sophie's voice drifts to us from the back seat. "Don't yell at Sierra. This is all my fault. Or at least Uncle Travis's," she amends. Then she begins to cry.

I give Levi a see-what-you've-done-now glare.

Levi glances up to the mirror, searching for Sophie. She's huddled miserably in a heap.

"Sophie." My throat tightens at the tenderness of his tone, and I forgive him for lecturing me. "None of this is your fault. In fact, Sophie, you are one of the bravest young women I've ever met."

Sophie sniffs. "So will you quit yelling at Sierra?"

Levi's mouth twitches in what I hope is amusement as two more fire trucks roar past us. "For now."

He gives me a look I interpret as "to be continued," but the tension eases between us and I settle back against the seat, eager to go home.

32

Saturday
November 23
7:00 p.m.

Sierra

W e reach Justice, and Levi turns onto the road leading to the McBride home. Nick keeps going straight.

"Hospital?" I ask.

"Yes. Jess's foot needs a doctor's attention right away. Nick said Sly and Maggie will meet them there." I'm shocked it is only seven o'clock. It feels like we lived a lifetime on that mountain.

Levi pulls my car into the driveway, and I'm not surprised to find Uncle Mal, Aunt Mary, and my mom all waiting for us on the open front porch. I climb out of the car and turn to help Sophie, but Levi is already there. My family surrounds Sophie and me and welcomes us home. We're bustled into the warmth of the living room as introductions and explanations swirl around us.

Aunt Mary positions herself near Sophie and gently lays her hand on the girl's shoulder. Sophie studies Aunt Mary's eyes for a moment, and whatever she sees there must reassure her. Brittle tension eases, and the furrow on Sophie's forehead smooths out for the first time since we were taken. Sudden tears sting my eyes as she slowly reaches for Aunt Mary and is gathered into her arms. Finally safe.

"WELL, I think she's settled in." Aunt Mary walks into the kitchen carrying Sophie's dirty clothes in a laundry basket. It had almost been funny to watch Sophie try to decide what she wanted first—food, a bath, or a bed. She eventually had all three.

"What's going to happen to her?" Mom puts a plate of cookies on the table and takes a seat beside me.

Aunt Mary glances at Uncle Mal. "I'm not sure. Nick still hasn't been able to locate her mother or uncle. They're likely hiding from the cartel. It would be a lot safer to turn themselves in to the police. Stealing drugs or money from the cartel is a death sentence."

My pulse increases as I consider how this could affect Sophie. "She can't go into foster care," I decree, panic rising in my voice.

"Sierra." Aunt Mary's calm tone reaches into my thoughts. "We didn't spend all this time looking for Sophie just to lose her again. God has a good plan for that young lady, so trust Him." She nods at Uncle Mal. "Trust us."

A weight lifts from my heart, and my exhaustion finally hits me. I'd planned to wait for a report from Cole or Nick on Jess's condition, but I can hardly keep my eyes open. To my relief, the back door opens, and Cole and Nick walk in, tired but calm.

"Jess?" I ask.

"She's doing okay," Cole responds as he walks to the refrigerator to forage for food. Aunt Mary joins him and points him to the table.

"You boys sit, and I'll make you some dinner."

Nick continues the report. "The doctor is keeping Jess

overnight for observation, but after he cleaned and re-bandaged her foot, he said she should be fine."

"Observation, ha," Cole mutters. "She needs full-time protection. From herself."

I'm struck by the tone of bitterness that flavors his words, and I wince, acknowledging my part in the decision to search for Sophie.

"Cole, I'm sorry," I say. "I should have said no to Jess."

Cole studies me, and I can see the moment he forgives me. "She can be very persuasive." He concentrates on the bowl of chili Aunt Mary places in front of him.

I study him, unable to shake the uneasy feeling Cole may have reached his limit with Jess. I hope not. It's clear he loves her.

Nick interrupts my thoughts by asking, "Where's Sophie? I'd hoped to ask her some questions tonight."

Aunt Mary lays her hand on Nick's shoulder. "She was beyond exhausted. I'm sure you'll do better talking to her tomorrow."

Nick nods and adds hot sauce to his chili before taking a bite. I watch to see if steam comes out of his ears, but he appears content with the level of heat as he practically inhales the food.

"Did you find out anything about Clive and his sister?" Uncle Mal asks.

Nick shakes his head. "No, there's no sign of them yet. But we put out an APB on the car they're driving, thanks to Sophie's description. We'll find them." He speaks those last words with finality.

I'm exhausted. I excuse myself. Thankfully, I showered the smoke out of my hair almost as soon as I got to the house.

Now I can go to the guest room, crawl into the bed, and sleep for about twenty hours. I say goodnight to my family and drag myself up the stairs.

The moon is shining, and it lights up the room as I walk to

the window to close the curtains. As I glance down, I notice Cole sitting on a bench in Aunt Mary's flower garden. The blooms are gone for the winter, and the picture strikes me as lonely and bleak. Roxie lies beside Cole, resting her head on his leg. Cole's head is down, and I can feel his sadness even from this second-story room. I fall asleep, my heart heavy with regret.

33

Sunday
November 24
10:00 a.m.

Jess

"I'm ready to go!" I sound like an irritable toddler, but I can't help myself. When I left the hospital after the gunshot and fever, I hoped I'd never come back until someone I loved had a baby. But less than seventy-two hours later, here I am.

"Be patient," Sly says impatiently. "The doctor will sign the release form, and we'll be out of here." She wanders into the hallway, probably to ask the nurse for a sedative for me, and maybe for herself too. Soon she returns waving a paper, sheer relief on her face.

"And we're out of here." She grabs the handles of my wheelchair and pushes. I hate the hospital rule about having to leave in a wheelchair, but today I'm a little relieved. My foot is throbbing, and I want to settle into Daddy's recliner with my foot propped up on a pillow.

We reach an elevator, and Sly pushes the button to take us

down to the parking lot. The doors open and Carl, the EMT, steps out. He pauses. "What's happening here?" he asks. "I thought Dr. Kennedy released you days ago. Did I miss an ambulance call?" There is jealousy in his voice.

"Carl, you know I'd never let anyone but you drive my ambulance."

Beside me, Sly emits an unladylike snort, but I ignore her. I give Carl a quick recap of last night's adventure, and he sends us on our way with an admonition of, "Try to stay out of trouble."

"I can't make any promises," I call out as the elevator door closes and we begin our descent.

Sly glares as I turn and smile at her.

"What?" I ask.

She shakes her head. "I don't know where to begin."

A weight of guilt swamps me at her words, but I'm too tired to discuss it right now. I just want to go home.

As I settle into Daddy's recliner, I'm amazed that less than twenty-four hours have passed since I sat here, waiting for Sierra and Grace to take me for a ride around town. Well, we definitely went on a ride. The kitchen door opens and closes, then Maggie bounces into the living room.

"You're home," she announces in delight. She leans over to give me a quick hug. "Cole dropped me off after church. I'm going to change clothes, then Rachel's mom is taking us to Lorrie's birthday party. 'Bye." She starts up the steps to her bedroom, but I stop her.

"Wait, Cole dropped you off?" I try not to sound hurt that he didn't come inside to visit me, but I fail.

Maggie doesn't meet my eyes when she explains, "He said he was running late for a meeting he had with Doc Anderson. They're going over some classes Cole will need next fall in college. He will stop by later, I'm sure."

She didn't say he said he'd stop by later. I give her my brightest fake smile and wave her on her way. "Yes, I'm sure he will."

Cole had this appointment already planned. Doc is helping him pick which classes to take when he registers at Montana University. Cole wants to be a livestock veterinarian, and he has the promise of a job with Doc after graduation.

Eventually, Cole will take over the practice. I'm excited about this next step for him, but the idea of him leaving in the fall is like a lead weight in the pit of my stomach. Now that increases as I consider Cole didn't stop to say hi to me before he headed for Doc's office.

Cole was beside me the entire time I was in the ER. Yes, he'd been quiet, but hey, it was a hospital, right? I drift off to sleep, uneasiness prickling my peace.

34

Sierra

The house is quiet when I wake up. I make my way downstairs and glance at the microwave clock. I slept until eleven thirty. I get out the peanut butter to spread on toast and rummage in the fridge for jam.

Behind me, Sophie asks, "Could I have some of that too?"

I grab the strawberry jam and turn to hug her. "Of course, you can! How did you sleep? You didn't have any nightmares, did you?"

Sophie stretches. "That's the best bed I've ever slept in. No nightmares." She reaches around me to grab a banana from a bowl on the counter. "But I'm starved."

"You've got a lot of missed meals to make up for." The toast pops up, and I slather peanut butter on one piece. "Jam?" I ask, holding up a clean knife. She nods, and I finish *cooking* our breakfast. I heat leftover coffee in the microwave and take my first sip. Uncle Mal makes the very best coffee. Sophie helps herself to some orange juice, and we settle at the table.

"Where is everybody?" she asks around a mouthful of PB and J toast.

"Church." I cut my toast into two triangles as Sophie stares.

"You know, you're kind of weird," she observes, and I nod in agreement.

We eat in companionable silence for a few minutes, then Sophie asks, "Do you think the cartel killed my mom and uncle?"

I choke a little on my swig of coffee. "Of course not. What makes you think that?"

Sophie shrugs. "Clive kept talking about how mad the cartel is about Travis stealing their drugs. He said even if the cartel doesn't kill him, Clive might." She appears to lose her appetite at the thought as she pushes the rest of her toast around on her plate.

I wish I knew what to tell her. My only knowledge of the cartel is from watching television, and how accurate can that be?

"We need to ask God to protect your mom and uncle. Nick and Levi are working with the FBI to find your family and make sure they're safe." I don't add that Travis will go to prison, but Sophie's a smart girl. She knows.

Car doors slam outside, and a moment later McBrides fill the kitchen. My mom comes straight to me and plants a kiss on the top of my head. Aunt Mary places a gentle hand on Sophie's shoulder.

"You girls sleep okay?" she asks.

We nod in unison, and she smiles, bustling to the pantry to pull out ingredients to make lunch. Sophie and I take our dirty dishes to the sink and rinse them before adding them to the dishwasher.

I catch Uncle Mal and Nick talking near the doorway, and I'm not surprised when Uncle Mal asks Sophie and me to join them in his office. Although Uncle Malcolm has his law office in a building in downtown Justice, his home office is also full of law books and other reference material.

Sophie and I settle into two chairs facing Uncle Mal's desk while he takes a seat in his leather office chair. Nick sits on the edge of the desk. It's weird to see him in anything besides his uniform. His boots, jeans, and sweater are all black, and he's as intimidating dressed for church as he is in uniform.

I wonder if Levi is working now or if he was at church. Sophie's hand reaches for mine and brings me back from my distracted thoughts.

Uncle Mal says, "Sophie, I spoke with Judge Elway this morning before church. He has granted Mrs. McBride and me temporary custody of you until your mom can be located. Is that acceptable?"

Sophie squeezes my hand. "Yes, I'd like to stay with you and Mrs. McBride."

Did I imagine that she whispered the word *forever*?

I turn to Nick. "Is there any progress in finding Clive and Maude?"

He straightens a little. "That's the reason we want to speak with you two. State troopers followed a tip about Clive's car sitting at a rest stop near Barretts. When they arrived, they found some blood in the car, but no Clive." Nick's voice is solemn.

Sophie gasps, and I grip her hand again. "What about Maude?" we ask in unison.

"No sign of her either." Nick shakes his head. "They are searching the area, since they're likely on foot."

"Or the cartel took them," Sophie suggests. "I kind of feel sorry for Maude. The kidnapping was Clive's deal, not hers. As mean as she was, I hate to think of the cartel getting her." Sophie's voice trails off, and she stands. "I'm exhausted. Is it okay if I go lay down again?"

"Sure," Nick says, and we all stand. We've only been here for five minutes. Such important news should take a lot longer to tell. But I guess the telling is quick. It's the processing that takes time. Clive and Maude are still out there, somewhere. I hope they are too busy running from the authorities and the cartel to think about coming after us. I follow Sophie upstairs, and we don't say a word as we go into our bedrooms. To process.

35

Sunday
November 24
1:00 p.m.

Jess

I 'm dozing in the recliner when I hear the back door open again, and I sit up. Cole?

No. It's Nick. Doing my best to maintain a neutral expression, I say, "Hi Nick."

I try not to let on he's the wrong McBride brother. Wrong for me, at least. After church, Sly came home and flew up the stairs to freshen up before he arrived.

"Jess." As usual, Nick is a man of few words.

He seems to be debating using a few more of them to address what happened. I brace myself for another lecture, but all he says is, "Got any big plans today?" His tone implies I should sit in this recliner all day.

I glance at the white bandage on my foot. It practically gleams. "Oh, I don't know," I say. "I thought I'd go dancing later."

Nick's lips twitch in an almost grin. "Still with the sass, I see."

"Forever."

He nods as if that is the answer he expected. "Fair enough."

Sly breezes in and, as they go out the door, I call after them, "Good talk, Nick." His chuckle lifts my spirits a little. Now, if his brother can be that understanding.

By four o'clock I've napped twice, read my daily devotional through next week, and watched a cooking show contest on television.

I'm yelling, "No, what are you thinking? That's way too much garlic," when Cole walks in the door. I feel the flush rise in my cheeks as I switch off the TV. I prepared an entire speech, but the expression on his face stops my words. And my heart.

He comes over to sit on the edge of the sofa. "How are you feeling?"

I want to say, "I'm scared. I'm sorry. Please forgive me." But I just say, "I'm okay."

He glances at my bandaged foot and nods. "They took care of you at the hospital." I kind of expect him to add *again*, but he doesn't. A wry smile tugs at his mouth. "We've been here before, haven't we?" I know he's referring to the risks I've taken.

I nod, but my throat is so full of tears I can't say anything.

"When you were in the hospital with the fever, I've never been so scared in my life. I thought," he chokes a little and tries again, "I thought I was going to lose you, Jess. I told myself I never wanted to feel that kind of fear again." He glances away to compose himself as tears sting my eyes.

"When you got out of the hospital, I thought, *Well, at least she'll be safe for a while.* Of course, I wasn't happy Rochelle shot you, but I guess I thought I'd have time to regroup. Recover from the trauma of watching you nearly slip away from me."

"When Nick called to tell me you were on your way to Bannack to rescue Sophie, I couldn't believe it. I thought he was pranking me. Nick and Levi picked me up at the stables. I kept looking for Sierra's car, possibly pulled off along the road. I told myself you would be waiting for us, that you wouldn't go into Bannack on your own. But when we saw the fire ..."

Cole stands and walks to the window, and when he turns back to face me, anger sparks for a moment in his eyes. I welcome the anger. At least I can understand anger.

But as quickly as it came, it's gone and my heart falls. This sad resignation is terrifying.

"I care about you, Jess. No, here's the truth, I'm in love with you. People say I'm too young for such a powerful emotion, but it's not a phase, or whatever they call it. I think I've been in love with you since you kicked me playing four square in grade school."

My tears are falling faster now.

Cole has never told me about that. I have a flash memory of getting off the bus that day, walking into the kitchen, and telling my mom, "I'm going to marry Cole McBride someday."

"Me too," I whisper, but if he hears me, he doesn't acknowledge it.

"I love you, Jess," he repeats my favorite words, but they are bittersweet. "But I can't be in your life that way anymore. We need to break up."

I think I knew the words were coming from the moment Cole walked in the door. But hearing them spoken is like a physical blow, and I sit back in the chair.

"You mean take a break?" I ask. Hoping. Praying that's what he means.

"No, I mean break up. I can't keep worrying about what's going to happen next. I need to focus on my classes. Graduation is only a few months away. Then I'll leave for college six weeks later. I've thought and prayed about this a lot over the past few days. I can't do this anymore, Jess. I can't do *us*."

Cole's eyes mirror my misery. He isn't doing this because he's mad or wants to teach me a lesson. I can almost hear our hearts break at the same time.

And then he's gone.

36

Monday
November 25
5:00 p.m.

Sierra

"Say that again," I demand.

"I don't want to," Grace mutters. "I hated saying it the first time." It's Monday afternoon, three days after the fire. Grace stopped by the McBride home after she dropped off Jess's schoolwork.

"Cole broke up with Jess," I say, the words sounding foreign to my ears. We're sitting in the overstuffed chairs on the enclosed porch. A space heater is running in the corner of the room, and while it's not toasty, the blankets we brought out with us make up the difference.

Roxie is sitting at my feet, patiently waiting for her guy to come home from work. At the mention of Cole's name, Roxie's ears perk up. I lean down and rub her neck, whispering, "Don't worry girl, Cole won't break up with you."

Sophie joins us and asks, "What's going on? Why do you look weird?" Weird is Sophie's word for anything out of the ordinary. I'm going to give that girl a thesaurus for Christmas.

"Cole broke up with Jess," Grace explains.

"No!"

I'm a little surprised by the vehemence in Sophie's reaction. But I remember the long hours she and I spent locked in the cabin. I'd passed the time telling Sophie about "The Adventures of Jess." When she heard about Jess's dream and how she'd been the one who figured out where Sophie was being held, Jess was forever elevated to hero status.

"Why would he do that?" Sophie demands, and Grace and I exchange a glance. "Because she went to Bannack to rescue me?" she asks in dismay and starts to cry.

I think of Levi's words to me as we drove down the mountain that night. *You were the adult in the car. You should have said no.*

"Sophie, it's not your fault at all," I say, my own tears falling.

Beside me, Grace sniffles. "I'm supposed to be the voice of reason to keep Jess in check. I should have insisted we wait for Nick."

The porch door opens, and Cole steps into the room. He's dusty from work, and his broad shoulders slump. He looks ... broken. For a moment he takes in the picture of Grace, Sophie, and me crying as we turn to glare at him.

Then he grimaces, but only shakes his head. "C'mon Roxie." Roxie, the traitor, follows him back outside.

Sophie jumps up and hurries toward the door. "I'm going to talk to him," she says, but I'm sure what she means is, "I'm going to yell at him until he apologizes to Jess and takes her lots of flowers and candy." At least that's what I'd say. But Grace and I reach up to grab her arm and tug her back to her chair.

"Not a good idea." Grace shakes her head. "Cole and Jess have to work this out on their own. We need to be supportive of Jess but not say anything negative about Cole."

At Sophie's frown, I say, "Cole has a right to protect himself from being hurt. He has a right to be happy."

"Humph," Sophie crosses her arms. "He doesn't look all that happy to me."

Grace and I glance at each other again, and I say, "No, he doesn't, does he?"

37

Tuesday
November 26
7:30 p.m.

Sierra

"You should stay out of it."

I'm on my first official date with Levi, and we're sitting in Leonardo's Italian Restaurant. I should be happy, but I can't stop worrying about Cole and Jess.

"I am. But you or Nick could talk to him ..." My voice trails off at Levi's horrified look.

"No way am I stepping into another guy's relationship problems. Even saying the words *relationship problems* feels wrong." Levi shudders, and I'm pretty sure he's not faking it. Despite the subject, I can't help but grin.

From what Levi has shared with me, he joined the army at age nineteen. He's seen combat in Afghanistan. He left the army after serving five years, the majority in special forces. Now he's a sheriff's deputy. But the idea of talking to Cole about Jess makes him practically break out in hives.

"You're right. You're probably not the best person to talk to Cole."

Quickly changing the subject, Levi asks, "How's Sophie doing?"

"She's good," I say, and I'm happy that is true. "She fits in with the McBrides like she was born there. It's only been three days, but she's already more at peace and less stressed."

Uncle Mal called Sophie's school in Dillon and explained the situation, and Nick brought her schoolwork home with him last night. Aunt Mary is helping her catch up, so she can rejoin her class after Thanksgiving.

Levi nods at the server when she asks if he wants more coffee. I was surprised and a little nervous when Levi said we were going to Leonardo's for our date. I knew that was where Cole and Jess and their friends had gone for homecoming a few weeks ago. Grace assured me it was a very special place.

Sly loaned me one of her outfits, a soft sweater dress in a muted pumpkin color and cream-colored half boots. She'd spent over an hour on my hair, making long blonde curls that fell over my shoulders and down my back. I've never felt prettier. I touch the topaz birthstone necklace at my throat. Nick made a point of returning it as soon as the forensics team finished the processing.

Last night, after I accepted Levi's invitation to dinner, I held the dog tags in my hands for a long time. I've worn them since I was eight years old. But over time, my purpose subtly changed from honoring my father to using them as a shield against pain. I thought they would remind me to never open my heart to anyone I might lose to a dangerous profession.

But life is unpredictable. I'll never have a guarantee of happily ever after, even if I fall in love with someone I consider "safe." I'd left the dog tags in my purse for the evening.

When Levi arrived tonight, wearing a gray T-shirt under a black sports coat and black jeans, I was a little overwhelmed. His blond hair has grown longer and is curling around his ears.

He laughed when he caught me looking at his hair. "Definitely not regulation," he said with a wink.

The server returns with a tray of desserts, bringing me back to the present.

Everything looks amazing, but I'm not hungry at all. I eat most of my salad and bread but only sample my ravioli. It's delicious, but I'm worried I might splash red sauce on Sly's dress, so I ask the server to box it up.

"Ready?" Levi asks.

"Almost," I say. "I want to stop at the ladies' room."

"Sure." He stands. "I'll bring the car around and pick you up out front."

I smile and make a beeline for the restroom.

As I lean over the sink to check my make-up in the mirror, another woman enters the bathroom. I'm so focused on what I'm doing that I don't look over, but that changes abruptly when I hear my name.

Maude blocks the door, pointing a gun at me. "Now, you'll be very quiet and do exactly what I say, or I'll shoot you. I got nothing left to lose."

Maude is a mess. Her shoes are muddy, the hem of her dress is torn, and she's wrapped in a man's sweater that's much too big for her. She oozes desperation.

"What do you want from me?" I try not to let my voice quiver, but there's a little squeak at the end of my words.

"Payback." Venom infuses the word.

"For what?" I ask, hoping to stall long enough for someone to see us.

"Clive's death. You didn't pull the trigger, but you might as well have. We were set to sell the girl and get the money to repay the cartel. Then we'd find that weasel Travis and kill him for what he did. If he hadn't stolen the drugs, none of this would have happened. But the cartel tracked us down. They got Clive while I was at the rest stop, and all I could do was watch from the shadows while they killed my brother."

She sniffs. "I took off, hot-wired me a truck so I had wheels. Following you tonight was easy." The gun begins to quake in her hand, but she catches me staring and grips it tighter. "Clive had me find out all about you when he first took you to the cabin, so I know about your rich lawyer uncle."

My thoughts race as I try to think of the best way to talk to Maude. Arguing with her is out—she has no conscience. The fact she was planning to help Clive sell Sophie to traffickers proves that. She said "payback," not revenge. Despite her declaration that she has nothing left to live for, I know she doesn't want to die or go to prison.

"How do you plan to get payback?" My heart is pounding so hard it almost drowns out my words.

"Your uncle is rich," she declares with such assurance I almost laugh. That's news to me, but I keep quiet.

"I've got a place to hide you while I wait for your uncle to pay a ransom. After I have the money, I'll take off and *forget* where I put you. Payback."

I resist rolling my eyes and fight to keep from saying, "Kidnapping, again? Because that worked out so well for you the other two times." I wisely keep my mouth shut.

Maude gives a wry smile before continuing, "Trust me, you won't be able to escape this time." There's something in her tone that makes me worry she may be right.

38

Tuesday
November 26
7:45 p.m.

Sierra

"Now, we're going out the back way. It's a few feet outside this door, and since I'll have this gun, you should keep quiet. If I have to shoot you, I might shoot a few other people too. Especially that guy you were with." At my start, she sneers. "Oh yeah, I followed you here. Snuck in the back door and waited for you to come back here to prettify yourself."

I grip my hands together to keep them from shaking as Maude opens the restroom door and motions me out into the short hallway. She's right, the back door is only steps away. Maude turns the handle on the door, and cool air rushes in. She nudges me with the barrel of the gun, and I step into the alley behind the restaurant. An outsized dumpster sits at one corner of the building, concealing us from the side parking lot.

Concealing us from Levi.

"I know where Cally Cat is," I say. I hate lying, so I'm glad I don't have to. Last night Cole told me a hunter had found a calico cat near Bannack Road. It was weak and injured, possibly from a fight with a raccoon. The hunter took it to Doc to treat its injuries. It had to be Maude's cat.

"Where?" I'm encouraged by the eagerness in Maude's voice. Maybe I can lure her out to Doc Anderson's and ... do what?

The good news is, we'll be away from others so she can't hurt anyone else. The bad news is, we'll be away from other people, and she can kill me if she wants to.

"She's being cared for at the vet's office on Bannack Road. Someone found her after you abandoned her Saturday night."

I can't resist the jab, but Maude counters with one of her own—the barrel of the gun.

"I didn't abandon her. She ran off, and Clive promised we'd hunt for her. Of course, he lied." Her words are bitter, and I have a sudden sense of sympathy for her. It evaporates quickly.

"How are we going to get out of here?" I ask, sudden hope stirring. If Maude stole a truck several days ago, then by now the owner will have called the authorities. They'll have the description and plate numbers.

Maude must read something in my face because she chortles, "Forget it, girlie. I dumped that truck and stole a different car." Pride infuses her words.

She nudges me with the gun, and we walk to the nearly empty parking lot. It's Tuesday night, so Levi and I'd had the restaurant mostly to ourselves. Sudden tears sting my eyes as I think of Levi, patiently waiting for me in front of the restaurant.

Quicker than I like, we're in the stolen car, with Maude driving. She keeps the gun trained on me as we pass other traffic, discouraging me from signaling to anyone. I scoot around on my seat and feel something poking into the back of my knee.

My phone! Sly had loaned me a small cream-colored clutch that almost matched my borrowed boots. It had a thin beaded strap that I'd looped over my wrist. I'd forgotten I had it, and Maude must have thought the strap was a bracelet. I glance at my current kidnapper, but she's busy navigating the back roads of Justice. Carefully, I tug my phone from the clutch. I'm relieved to see Levi was the last person I texted when I confirmed the time for our date tonight.

I hold the phone down by my side nearest the car door, where Maude can't spot it. Then I open the app and frantically think of what to text. A memory flashes and I quickly type, "Knucklehead. Vet." Then I hit send.

I hope Levi recognizes the knucklehead reference. Otherwise, he'll think I'm an idiot and never ask me out again. That's not my first concern here, though. I bite my lip and try to appear scared, which isn't hard to do.

"Tell me how to find Bannack Road," Maude demands.

"Do you want to go through town, or take side streets to avoid possible police cars?" I ask, trying to appear innocent. She tosses me a suspicious frown. "I don't want anyone else to be hurt." The honesty in my voice reassures her.

"Back roads," she orders, and I take her on an extended tour of Justice. We've been meandering through neighborhoods for over twenty minutes when Maude finally snaps, "Let's get on with it. Stop your stalling." She glares at me, and I don't have a choice.

"Take the next right and go to the stop sign. Turn left on First Street, and it will take us straight to Bannack Road."

She eyes me suspiciously but follows my directions. In minutes we've left the relative safety of Justice and are traveling up the mountain on Bannack Road. I pray Levi received my text and understood the meaning.

Sooner than I'd like, we're pulling into the empty parking lot of Doc's clinic. I'm disappointed his truck is missing from its usual parking spot. On the other hand, I'm relieved he won't be in danger too. Maude parks right at the entrance of the building and checks around nervously. "Get us inside."

I raise my eyebrows in dismay. "How am I supposed to do that? I don't have a key."

She uses the gun to motion me toward the door, where she examines the lock then stands back and shoots. It's so fast, I scarcely have time to jump back as shards of metal fly through the air. Maude rattles the lock, and I'm not sure which of us is more surprised when the door swings open.

"Move." Maude nudges me with the barrel of the gun, and I feel the heat in my back from the recent discharge. We walk into the clinic. I've only been here once with Cole, so I'm not sure where Maude's cat is being kept. It's dark except for a security light near the reception area. I reach for the light switch but Maude snarls, "No."

She digs in the pocket of her sweater and pulls out a small flashlight. After flipping the button, she swings the beam around until she spots a door marked *kennel.* Once again, she digs the gun into my ribs and urges me to the door. "That way."

The space is compact with only five cages of varying sizes. Doc is a livestock vet, so he does most of his work at the ranches. All the cages are empty except for two.

In the first cage is an animal that is larger than a cat or even most dogs. But the dim light makes it hard to see what it is. A second later a loud bleat echoes around the room. I jump back, startled, but peer closer at a goat.

Maude ignores the goat in favor of the cage at the end of the row. She hurries over and kneels, crooning, "Cally Cat, you naughty kitty. I've been looking everywhere for you."

I glance around the room, looking for any weapon I can use, but Maude glares at me. "Find the key to this cage. Now."

She holds the gun in her right hand, and I can't escape until she is better distracted.

As my eyes adjust to the dimness of the room, I notice the keys hanging on the wall next to the door. I debate hiding the key. As soon as Maude has her cat, she's either going to stash me while she waits for Uncle Mal to bring the ransom, or shoot me. I'm not a fan of either option.

As I reach for the key, a firm hand covers my mouth, and an

arm wraps around my waist. I struggle but there's no give from my captor. I'm lifted off my feet and pulled back into the reception room.

"Sierra, it's me. Levi. Be very quiet."

My heart lurches and I give a slight nod. Levi removes his hand from my mouth as Maude screeches, "Where did you go? Come back here!"

Levi nudges me toward the front door. "Go outside and wait for Nick."

Before I can respond, he turns and reaches into a holster strapped to his side. He pulls out a gun and peeks around into the entrance to the kennel. If he's surprised by the bleating of the goat, he doesn't react.

I'm frozen in the place where Levi left me. Yes, he wants me outside and away from danger, but I can't seem to move. Chancing a quick peek around the doorframe, I'm surprised to only spot Maude. She's waving the gun around, frantically looking for a target. Probably me. Levi has faded into the shadows. The noise is raucous with Maude shouting, Cally hissing, and the goat bleating.

It would almost be funny if it wasn't so terrifying.

Maude barrels through the doorway and I jump back, regretting my decision to stay in the building. "There you are." There's a new menace in Maude's eyes. If I thought her reunion with her cat would soften her, I was wrong. I hope I'm not dead wrong.

"I-I was looking for the key," I stammer. Behind Maude, I notice a movement and I try to keep my focus on Maude, as Levi materializes from the shadows. I can read the frustration in his eyes. If he moves toward Maude, she might shoot me, either by accident or on purpose. Either way, I could be dead.

Levi nods sharply toward the reception counter located

about two feet from where I stand. I take a leap and land, hard, on the tile floor behind the counter. As I'm airborne, Maude raises her gun and Levi snaps, "Drop the weapon, Maude. You're under arrest."

I peek over the counter. Levi is standing with his gun in Maude's back, encouraging her to give up. In the dim light, I can make out the indecision in Maude's eyes as she considers her options.

My heart pounds, and I feel nauseated.

She could still turn and fire at Levi.

"Drop it!" Levi's words are sharp, and after a terror-filled second, Maude holds out her hand and lets the gun clatter to the floor.

He holsters his gun and reaches into his pocket, pulling out zip ties, kind of random but definitely handy. He binds Maude's hands behind her back.

"You came prepared." I nod toward Maude, who is rolling her shoulders and glaring.

"Always," he says with a grin. "I grabbed them out of my glove box on my way in." He studies my face. "You okay?"

I give a quick nod, stand on shaky legs, and lean against the counter.

The next few minutes are a blur as Levi recites Maude's Miranda rights. Nick comes through the front door, gun unwavering. But when he sees the danger is past, he puts his weapon away and says, "I thought you were going to wait for backup?"

"There wasn't time," Levi says.

Maybe I can use that excuse for why I didn't go outside. It's worth a try. Levi ushers Maude through the door and puts her in the back of Nick's squad car.

"Wait," Maude wails. "What about my Cally Cat?"

I step forward and say, not unkindly, "Don't worry Maude. I'll take very good care of her."

39

Sierra

At the sheriff's office, Nick takes my statement while Levi escorts Maude to booking. Soon the room fills with deputies, Justice police officers, and FBI agents. When I notice the FBI insignia, I think of Jess's dream of joining them one day. The thought of Jess sends a wave of guilt and sadness through me.

I'm not responsible for what has happened over the past few weeks, but I can't shake the guilt. Poor Jess. From the beginning, she only tried to help, from finding me on the road after I escaped from Clive to trying to catch Leopard Woman and Rochelle, to trying to rescue Sophie. Her intentions were good. But Rochelle shot her, she almost died from an infection, nearly burned up in a fire, and lost Cole. It's not fair.

I tell Nick everything that's happened tonight. His only

reaction during the entire story is at the beginning when I tell him Levi and I were on a date. He raises a dark eyebrow and studies me before looking down at the report.

"Go on," is all he says.

As I finish relating the events of the night, there's a commotion at the front of the room. Nick stands and says, "Give me one minute," then he joins the crowd of FBI agents gathered in a corner. One minute turns into ten, but when he returns, satisfaction shows on his face.

"Sophie's mom, Lydia Granger, and her Uncle Travis just turned themselves in to the FBI. Travis heard through his connections that the cartel killed Clive. He figured prison might be safer."

"Did Lydia break the law?"

"Hard to say yet." Nick picks up his pen and clicks the end, signaling it is time to finish the report. I sigh at Nick's reticence. I'll try to learn more information from Levi later.

The thought of Levi seems to make him materialize. "You almost done?" he asks Nick.

"Just finishing up," Nick says.

"I need to talk to Sheriff Herman, then I'll be back for Sierra."

"No need, I'm heading home in a few, and I can take her with me."

"That's okay," Levi says, putting a hand on Nick's shoulder. "We need to finish our date."

Nick stands, and I'm afraid he's going to say I can't go with Levi. Anger flares at his presumption, but all he says is, "Fair enough."

Ten minutes later, I'm once again sitting next to Levi in his car. I glance down at Sly's dress, relieved it survived this latest adventure fairly well. I took advantage of the time Levi spent with Sheriff Herman to go to the ladies' room to fix my hair and make-up, at least the best I could.

Levi is quiet as we leave the sheriff's department parking lot. The drive will only take five minutes, so I hope he talks soon.

"You did good tonight." Of all the things I expected Levi to say, that wasn't on the list. I flush a little at the compliment and the warmth increases as he says, "I'm proud of you."

Sudden tears sting my eyes, but I resist the urge to turn away. "Thank you," I whisper.

He chuckles. "That knucklehead text was genius."

I glance down shyly but smile. "I hope I didn't offend you."

"No. I'd been getting uneasy when you didn't come out of the restaurant. I went inside and sent someone into the restroom to find you.

The manager returned and said no sign of you, but the back door was open. I realized someone had taken you." His look is solemn. "I prayed it wasn't the cartel."

I shudder at the thought. Words catch in my throat as I try to speak. "Thank you for coming after me. Thank you for saving my life."

Levi's voice is gruff with emotion. "I just found you. I didn't want to lose you."

A moment later, he parks in the driveway and comes around to open my door. He takes my hand as we walk up to the front porch. Then he turns me to face him, places his hands on either side of my face, and tilts it up. My breath catches as he leans down to kiss me.

This kiss is a revelation.

I've been kissed before, but those were the tentative kisses of a boy. There is nothing tentative about Levi Cooper's kiss.

When he lifts his head, I'm embarrassed by my mewl of protest. He draws me closer and rests his lips on my forehead. Then, too soon, he moves back and opens the door of the screened porch. He uses his finger to lift my chin and leans down for another quick kiss on my lips. "Good night, Sierra."

Turning, I step onto the porch, feeling his gaze on me as I

walk to the kitchen door. I glance back over my shoulder. "Levi, I ..." I begin, having no words to say.

In the moonlight, I catch his wink as he says with a smile, "I'm aware."

40

Jess

My fingers shake as I try to hook Mama's gold cross necklace around my neck. After three tries, it catches and dangles at the neckline of my raspberry-colored sweater. I'd let Maggie practice her French braiding again, and I'm glad there are fewer bobby pins this time.

I add a bit of blush to my too-pale cheeks and use the lipstick Sly found for me at the mall. It matches my sweater exactly. My plaid skirt carries the same shade of raspberry and I'm wearing my tan boots with deep pink embroidered flowers stitched on the sides. I look as good as I can, at least on the outside. I hope the outfit will disguise the fact that my heart is breaking.

I'd already been dreading spending Thanksgiving with the McBride family. I haven't seen or spoken to Cole in five days, ever since he told me he was done. We were done. That's the longest time I've ever gone without at least texting him. Even before we were a couple, we talked almost every day. The silence is deafening.

"We don't have to go, you know," Sly offered several times. "We can do our own Thanksgiving here, just you, Maggie, and me." Her offer touched me. I knew she would sacrifice the holiday with Nick to protect me. But I have to face Cole sometime. At least today I will do it looking my best.

Sly carries the casserole dish filled with sweet potatoes as Maggie helps me down the front steps and to the Honda. "You look beautiful, Jess," Sly says as she sets the casserole on the floorboard in the back.

Maggie slides into the backseat. "Yeah, that'll show Cole what he's missing."

"Margaret!" Sly's use of Maggie's full name shows her dismay at our little sister's words. "That's not helpful. You'll be as nice to Cole as you ever are, understand me?"

"He's a jerk," Maggie mutters, and Sly continues to glare at her. I look down, stifling a brief smile at Maggie's characterization of Cole. It kind of warms my heart to have her defend me.

But Sly is right. "Magpie, I appreciate your loyalty," I say, glancing at her in the mirror. "But the McBrides have always been kind to us, and I don't want to ruin this for them. Okay?" Maggie nods, and soon the Thomas sisters are on our way to Thanksgiving dinner.

The temperatures have dropped in the past few days, so there's no impromptu football game on the front lawn as we arrive. I remember the celebration we had here a few weeks ago, and my heart aches even more. Cole had brought Roxie home from Doc Anderson's after she recovered from wounds caused by the cougar, Outlaw. At least I have that sweet memory to cherish.

The delicious smell of roasting turkey greets us at the

kitchen door. Sly joins Mary and Sierra's mom, Connie, to help with the meal prep. Maggie helps me hobble through the dining room and into the living room, where Nick and Malcolm are watching the football game. Nick spots us first and jumps up to offer his seat. The compassion in his eyes almost undoes me, and I'm relieved when I hear Sierra's voice behind us.

"Jess, let's go to my room and catch up. And Maggie, Sophie is waiting for you upstairs." Sierra helps me hobble up the steps and we head for Piper's old bedroom. Maggie separates from us at the top of the steps when she sees Sophie and the two girls hurry off, talking so fast it's surprising they can understand each other.

Sierra settles me in a wingback chair near the window and drags an ottoman over to prop under my foot.

"You look amazing," Sierra says.

I nod my thanks but jump right to the point. "Is he going to be here?"

Sierra doesn't pretend to misunderstand. "Yes, he went to pick up more ice." I look away, wishing I hadn't asked. Sierra sits on the edge of the ottoman and says, "Jess, he's miserable."

Tears sting my eyes. I don't want Cole to be miserable. I just want him to be mine again. "Let's talk about something else." We spend the next minutes catching up on what happened to Sophie's mom and Travis.

"Uncle Malcolm is working with child protection services and Judge Elway. Lydia, Sophie's mom, is being charged with child abandonment. So far, there's no proof she was involved with the drugs or cartel. But considering she allowed Travis to live with them and buy and sell drugs from her home, she'll have to work hard to get Sophie back."

"Will the McBrides let her stay here?"

"Yes, they're taking steps to be foster parents for Sophie."

I'm relieved. Not only will Sophie be out of that destructive environment, but she'll be with the most stable family I know.

We're interrupted by Nick's shout of "Dinner" that echoes up the stairs.

Sierra sees the panic in my eyes and says, "Sophie and I set the table. You'll sit between us, and Cole will be far down the table." She helps me to my feet and hands me my cane.

"Don't worry, I'll be right with you the whole time, I promise." She leads me down the stairs and into the dining room.

As expected, the table is beautiful, set with Mary's best china and sparkling glassware. I can't believe the table isn't sagging with the weight of all the food.

I hold my breath, anticipating seeing Cole for the first time in five days. He's sitting at the opposite end of the table, talking to his Aunt Connie. I settle into my seat and take a lot of time looking at my lap as I unfold my napkin.

The chatter dies down, and Malcolm says, "Let's thank God for all of His blessings, and also for this delicious food."

I glance up to catch Cole watching me with such sadness, I almost break. I want to run away from the table, away from this house. Away from the hurt. As soon as they say the amens, a glob of stuffing lands on my plate, startling me.

Sophie grins. "I'm going to be your server today."

On the other side of Sophie, Maggie sends me a smile, and I need to stop feeling sorry for myself. Over the next few minutes, I'm caught up in several conversations with Sophie, Maggie, and Sierra. I feel like there is an invisible wall of protection around me, and I'm grateful.

When the meal is over, I've only looked at Cole one other time. I'd raised my chin and met his eyes without looking away. He gave me an almost imperceptible nod and resumed eating his dinner. I'll dissect that nod when I'm alone tonight, but right now I'm determined to show I'm strong and moving on.

As the meal ends, Sierra's mom stands and taps a fork against her water glass. "I have so much to be thankful for today," she says. Tears glisten in her eyes as she continues. "God protected our young women and returned them safely to us. But there's another reason to celebrate. Sierra is twenty years old today. Happy birthday, sweetheart!"

I turn as my friend accepts the good wishes, knowing how special this day is to her. Sierra told me that there were several times over the last few weeks she'd questioned if she would be around to celebrate her birthday. Malcolm enters the room carrying a beautifully decorated birthday cake, and soon we are enjoying our dessert. Pumpkin pie will have to wait until later.

As people take their plates into the kitchen for clean-up, I'm excused from kitchen duty because of my foot, so I make my way to the living room. It's empty for the moment, and I consider turning the television back on, anticipating the next football game.

But what I need is peace. I slip into the small room that Mary calls her reading nook. It opens to the living room on one end, and the enclosed porch on the other. A small white bookcase sits beside a cozy chair and I'm scanning titles for something to read when I hear a knock at the front door. I begin hobbling across the small room, disappointed my time of privacy has been interrupted.

But before I can step into the living room, Cole walks through it and opens the front door. His back is to me, so he doesn't see I'm nearby.

But his visitor does.

41

Thursday
November 28
Thanksgiving Day
4:00 p.m.

Jess

Amy Sinclair sweeps in, holding a pie pan. Her eyes widen when she sees me standing in the doorway of the smaller room, and a sly smile shows on her bright red lips.

"Cole, Happy Thanksgiving," she coos, holding out the pie like it's made of gold. "I overheard you talking to Josh at the stables. Remember the other day, when we were working together after school?" Amy breezes on without waiting for a reply. "You mentioned you love lemon meringue pie, so I worked all afternoon cooking this for you."

Cole takes the pie cautiously like he thinks it may explode. He sets it on a side table and says, "Um, thank you, Amy. That was very ... umm, thoughtful of you."

If Amy made that pie, I'll eat ... well, I don't know what I'll eat, but it won't be the pie. She doesn't even understand you bake a pie, not cook it.

I step forward to send Amy on her way, but I don't have that right anymore. Cole broke up with me.

Amy taunts me with a self-satisfied smile and continues. "I've really enjoyed working with you this week, Cole. Bob says I'm doing such a good job he may not need Jess anymore."

Amy is a force of nature, and it's clear she's making her statements for my benefit, not Cole's. She's hardly given him a chance to say a word. I'd thought Amy and I had resolved our feud. But since Cole is free now, it looks like all bets are off. I'm sick at the thought of Amy working with Cole. Doing my job. With my boyfriend.

"Amy," Cole begins, but before he can say anything else, Amy sends me a triumphant look and stands on tiptoe to link her arms around Cole's neck. Then she pulls his head down to hers and kisses him.

I awkwardly stumble back into the book room, then worry Cole might have heard me. It's bad enough that Amy knows I saw that kiss. I turn and, with little grace, I almost fall through the door onto the porch. I don't stop there but stagger down the outside steps, terrified I'll fall.

The night air is chilly against my flushed cheeks as I go to Sly's car. I don't have the keys, and even if I did, my bandaged foot would prevent me from driving. I debate about trying to walk home, but the throbbing in my foot changes my mind. Instead, I climb into the back of the Honda, tip over onto the back seat, and sob.

———————

SOPHIE AND MAGGIE find me asleep in the car. By the time they locate Sly, and she turns on the heater, my teeth are chattering. Sly says nothing about how dumb it was for me to do this. She tells Maggie to say goodbye to Sophie, and then we're on our way home.

When I'm wrapped up like a mummy in two blankets, Sly settles on the bed beside me and smooths my hair back from my temples. The braid Maggie worked so hard on has unraveled, and that makes me unbearably sad.

"Want to talk about it?" she asks.

"No."

She doesn't argue but pulls me closer and lets me lean my head on her shoulder. "Do you want me to talk about it?" She suppresses a tiny smile when I look at her in horror.

"No, please."

"That's best anyway since I'm not sure I'd know what to say."

"Mamma would," I respond and immediately feel guilty. "Not that you don't have good advice ..." My words trail off.

"You're right," Sly agrees, and I'm not sure which statement she's responding to. Maggie slips into the room and arranges herself at my back, wrapping her slight arms around my middle.

"I miss Mamma and Daddy," Maggie says. "Sometimes it's hard to be orphans."

Sly meets my eyes in concern. Maggie has never used that word before. Orphans. We're all quiet for a while, then I surprise us all by saying, "I will not leave you as orphans."

"That's from the Bible, right?" Maggie asks.

"Yes, it's the verse for next Friday in my devotional." At their puzzled expressions, I explain, "I read ahead."

"That reminds me of a song based on a scripture in John" Sly says. "I think the words are:

I will not leave you as orphans
I will come to you
I've engraved you on the palm of my hand
And I make all things new"

I settle onto my pillow, comforted by the words and the faithful love of my sisters. Whatever happens, God will be with us.

42

Sierra

"I thought I'd find you out here." Levi joins me on the loveseat. The memory of his kiss the other night makes my cheeks flush and I try to disguise my rapid breathing.

"I needed some alone time," I admit. During dinner, I was proud of Jess. She'd talked with Sophie and me, and even managed a few genuine laughs. But something happened to send her out into the night alone.

I have a feeling Cole is responsible somehow, and I hurt for them both. Levi settles beside me, and guilt flashes as if I don't have a right to be happy. Jess would hate for me to feel like that, and I brush it away.

Having Levi this close is overwhelming, and I hope he can't hear my heart pounding. He's still in his uniform, so I ask, "Are you finished for the evening or on dinner break?"

"Just a quick break," he says. "Mrs. McBride is making me a turkey sandwich and some pumpkin pie to take back on patrol." Levi reaches into his jacket pocket and brings out a small gift bag decorated with lovely pastel rosebuds. "Happy birthday." He hands me the bag. I'm startled, since I hadn't mentioned my birthday to him, but he quickly explains with a smile, "Sly."

With a shy smile, I reach into the bag to pull out a tissue-wrapped box. I unwrap it and give a delighted squeak. The teal box looks like a tiny suitcase complete with a cream-colored handle and lock. On the top are the words, "You make known to me the path of life, Psalm 16:11."

"Do you like it?" I'm surprised by the concern in Levi's voice, but when I look up, he relaxes. My face must say it all.

"I love it." Impulsively, I lean over to hug him. "Thank you."

He smiles in relief and draws me closer, placing a soft kiss on my temple. "Good. I wish I had more time tonight," he says, almost to himself, and leans his head back against the cushion.

I glance at him and recognize vulnerability. His mood has shifted, and unease skitters through me. My heart rate speeds up, if that's possible. I have the sense the rest of our conversation is important. I also have the sense I may not like the outcome.

"Levi?" I reach out to touch his hand, then draw back.

"I need to tell you something," he says, facing me. Now I'm sure I won't like what's coming. In the history of time, those words, spoken in that tone, have never been good news.

"What is it?" I try to make my voice steady, but the words end with a tiny squeak.

"I've been recalled."

"You're defective?" As soon as I make the joke, I regret it, but Levi's lips twitch.

"Not exactly. I've been recalled to active duty for a special mission."

Unreasonable anger surges through me. "They can't do that.

You are out of the army. Done. Finished. Who do they think they are, thinking they can have you back?"

I'm vibrating with anger ... and fear. I reach up to touch my dog tags but they aren't there. Irrationally, I panic as if they will protect me from what is coming next.

"I guess they think they're the government," he responds with a wry smile. "I always knew this was a possibility, but I didn't expect it to come this soon."

"You knew it was a possibility." Now I focus my anger on Levi. I want to demand answers. Why didn't he mention this before? The rational part of my mind says we aren't a couple. Yet. The past two weeks have held a promise of potential.

But Levi had no obligation to tell me, especially since the situation surprised him too. Unreasonable or not, hurt tightens my voice when I ask, "When do you have to leave?"

He doesn't answer right away, and I have a glimmer of hope. It's possible he won't leave for a few months. I've been concerned about having a long-distance relationship when I return to Missoula in January. If he stays through the holidays, we'll have time to build a closer relationship.

"Sierra." Levi catches my hand with a gentle squeeze. "Tomorrow."

43

Jess

"Hi there, can I come in?" Sierra calls from the kitchen. I sit up straighter and stretch my legs on the couch.

Sly delivers my visitor. "Sierra brought lots of leftovers from dinner last night. I'll put them away, unless you're hungry?" Sly has been trying to tempt me with food all day.

"No thanks." I have a brief memory of the lemon meringue pie Amy delivered to Cole and hope that's not in the care package Sierra brought.

Sierra sits in Daddy's recliner, facing me. "How are you?"

This question has been on my mind all day. I don't want to lie, but I don't want to ruin Sierra's mood. She was looking forward to seeing Levi during his break yesterday, so instead of answering her question, I ask one of my own.

"Did you and Levi talk last night?" I smile with genuine warmth, letting my happiness for Sierra show on my face.

But to my shock, her cheerful façade crumples, and she starts to cry. "He's leaving," she sobs.

"Who's leaving?" Grace comes through the living room door with a plate of turtle brownies. "Sly sent these in." She places the snowman-shaped plate on the coffee table.

"Levi." Sierra appears embarrassed about her reaction as she reaches for a tissue box on an end table.

"Why?" I ask.

"Where?" Grace says.

"He's been called for a mission with his special ops group." Sierra sniffles and touches the tissue to her nose.

For a minute, I'm distracted by how ... delicately she cries. When I cry, my eyes and face become red and blotchy. The only sign Sierra has been crying is a lone teardrop touching her long lashes. Cole has long lashes like hers. I shake my head and focus. This crisis isn't about me. For once.

"Wait," Grace frowns. "I thought Levi was out of the army."

"Apparently, there's a clause that allows them to call him back for a short time." I detect a slight trace of bitterness in Sierra's voice.

"How short a time?" I ask.

She shrugs. "He doesn't know, and he can't tell me where he's going or what he's doing. But I assume it's dangerous." She begins to cry again.

"When does he leave?" I ask.

"Tonight."

"Oh no," I blurt out, then stammer, "Well, I mean, the sooner he leaves, the sooner he will come back, right?"

Sierra doesn't seem to have heard me, which is just as well. "I'm going back to Missoula in the middle of January, when classes start again. But I thought we'd have time together during Christmas break. Instead, I'll be here without him." She clears her throat. "Okay, that's enough of this pity party. Let's talk about something else."

Sierra and Grace look at me expectantly, and I shake my

head. "No. No way. I'm not going there." I read relief in their expressions, and I don't blame them. One heartbroken friend is enough for now.

"I want to tell you something," Grace's tone is serious, and Sierra and I exchange a startled look.

"Please be good news," Sierra breathes, and I nod.

"I think this qualifies," Grace says thoughtfully. "Do you remember when we were trying to climb out of the window?"

"You mean when the fire was about two feet away and we thought we were going to burn to death?" I ask. "That time?"

Grace manages a small smile, but it's obvious she has something important to share. "So, you two were pulling on my arms but I couldn't jump high enough to make it through the window."

I shudder, thinking of the panic I'd felt.

Grace's voice is thick with tension. "I thought I was going to die. Then I remembered that Jess and I had talked about the Bible story of Shadrach, Meshach, and Abednego. How Jesus was in the fire with them."

Sierra and I nod, and I reach for Grace's hand, sensing the weight of her words.

"I never could have jumped high enough for you to pull me through the window. But then," Grace looks away, tears sliding down her cheeks. "I felt someone lift me up and almost toss me through the window." Her words come out in a rush, as she watches for our reaction.

"We know," Sierra says quietly, and I nod.

"You know?" Grace squeaks.

"Yes, we talked about it later," I explain. "You came flying through that window so fast, it couldn't have been just our strength. You had to have help from your guardian angel."

"Why didn't you say something before this?" Grace asks.

"We were going to," Sierra says. "But sometimes things mean more when you figure them out on your own. We didn't want to take that away from you."

Grace gives us a grateful smile. "Thank you."

We sit for a long time, thinking about that night and what we might have lost.

But God.

"Well, Christmas is coming." Grace reaches for a brownie and takes a delicate bite. "Have you started shopping?"

"Maggie is at the Black Friday sales with Rachel's family today. They left at 5:00 a.m." I shudder at the thought.

"I can't think of anything I need enough to wake up that early," Grace says.

"Mom and I are planning to drive up to campus next weekend to pick up some of my winter clothes. We are going to the outlet mall on the way. You two are welcome to come with us," Sierra offers.

Grace accepts, but I decline. "I'm going to do most of my shopping online this year." I nod at my bandaged foot.

"How long will you have the cast?" Grace asks.

"Hopefully just a few weeks."

"Oh good, you should be fine when we go to the winter retreat over Christmas break."

"A retreat sounds kind of fun," Sierra says, and Grace turns to her.

"You should come too." Grace's eager smile accompanies the invitation. "It's for our junior and senior high school groups at church. But college students sometimes come along to chaperone since they're on winter break."

At Sierra's hesitant expression, I chime in. "C'mon Sierra. Do you honestly want to stay around Justice when all the fun people are away?"

Sierra smiles. "Well, when you put it that way. But if Levi gets back before then, I'll be staying here."

"Well, duh." Grace and I laugh together.

Grace checks her phone. "Well, I need to run. I promised Mrs. Ellison I'd watch the twins while she goes shopping." She leans down to give me a hug then hurries to the door.

"Remember who is in charge," I call after her.

"Janey?" Grace's laugh follows her out the door.

My smile fades as I catch Sierra regarding me with a frown creasing between her brows. "Jess, I understand you don't want to talk about Cole, but can you tell what happened last night? There has to be a reason you spent an hour in a freezing car." Her concern is so genuine I blink away quick tears.

"Amy Sinclair stopped to give Cole a pie. She saw me, but Cole didn't, and she used the opportunity to talk about how they're working together at the stables now." I push down the hurt.

"Oh, that Amy," Sierra growls in a tone that doesn't express fondness.

"That's not the worst part." Now the floodgates are open, and I need to tell it all. "Amy and Cole k-kissed." I stammer, then look away so Sierra can't observe the depth of my pain.

"What?" Sierra leaps up so fast I move back. "I can't believe that! Well, I can believe it about Amy, but not Cole. Are you sure of what you saw?"

I knead a tissue in my hand and nod miserably. "Yes."

Sierra paces the room. "Oh, wait until I see my cousin," she threatens.

"No!" I almost jump from my seat but remember my foot. "Please, Sierra, don't. I couldn't stand it if Cole knew I was eavesdropping."

"Were you?"

"No, I guess not. I was in the reading area off the living room, looking for a book. It was just bad timing." I swallow my tears. "Maybe it was good I saw it. Now I won't sit here hoping Cole will change his mind. It really is over."

Sierra kneels in front of me and takes my hands in hers. "Jess, I am so sorry you are going through this."

I can tell she wants to offer more, but what is there to say? I give her a watery smile and change the subject. "I've been thinking about something,"

Sierra settles at the end of the couch, ready to listen.

"I've seen myself through the lens of being with Cole. Even before we were *us*, we were the closest of friends. I have wonderful memories of our times together at the winter retreat. It stings to know I won't be making more memories with Cole." I look away, considering my next words.

"But I've realized something important. I need to discover *Jess* again. I need to explore who I am. Who I want to be. Cole hasn't purposely stopped me from doing that, but now I have the time to focus on what comes next. For me."

Sierra regards me thoughtfully. "I think that's the smartest thing I've heard in a long time. In fact, I need to do that too. Instead of feeling sorry for myself, missing Levi, I'll use the time to discover myself."

I smile. "You'll find out you're a pretty amazing person all on your own."

Sierra stands and leans down for a hug. "So will you."

After Sierra leaves, I continue to think about our conversation as I sample a brownie. I've always loved the verse, Jeremiah 29:11 that says, "I know the plans I have for you, says the Lord. Plans to prosper you and not to harm you. Plans to give you hope and a future."

I'm not sure what my future with Cole will look like. There's a deep ache when I think about him never being in my life again. But God promises He has a plan, and I choose to trust Him.

I smile at those words.

"But God."

I drift off, the brownie still in my hand.

44

Friday
November 29
6:00 p.m.

Sierra

L evi pulls me close for a hug and places a soft kiss on the top of my head. I raise my face for another, but he just smiles. "I'll kiss you again when I come home." We're standing on the screened porch I consider "our spot." Inside, the McBride family is gathering to send Levi off with prayer.

"Let's go." Levi leads me into the living room, gently gripping my hand in his.

"Ah, here they are now." Uncle Mal opens his arms to draw us into the circle, and I blush to think they've been waiting for us to have our private goodbye. "Levi, we want to send you off with a prayer of blessing and protection," Uncle Mal says, and my throat tightens as the word *protection* emphasizes the danger. My heart skitters, and I know I'm taking a giant step forward in trusting God.

Sometimes I say the words, but they're almost an

afterthought, not acknowledging the power of the statement. Tonight I feel the weight of them settling into peace in my heart.

"Dear Father, we send Levi out to fulfill his assignment. We ask that You surround him and go before him. We trust You to being him home safely to us." Uncle Mal asks God for wisdom for the officers in charge. Aunt Mary prays for the soldiers Levi will be with on the assignment. Several others pray, too, and I glance around the room, my heart full of gratitude at their care for Levi.

My mom is holding my other hand, and next to her are Aunt Mary and Uncle Malcolm. Sly is next to my uncle and holds hands with Nick. Maggie and Sophie nestle in between Nick and Levi and I'm happy Sophie has found a safe place here.

Cole and Jess are the only ones missing. Cole is working late tonight, and Sly confided that she hated to wake Jess to join us. Their absence leaves an empty place in this family gathering.

"Amen." Everyone speaks the word, sealing the prayer for Levi. As the family shares their goodbyes with Levi, I study each of them, overwhelmed by love so sharp it almost stings. Trusting God to protect the people we love is hard. But that's the only way to have peace.

MEOW. Cally nudges my arm, and I reach over to smooth her soft fur. She and Roxie have a fragile agreement to share the house, but Cally prefers to stay close to me. From the window in Piper's room, I watch the taillights of Levi's car as he leaves for his next assignment. Reaching for the keepsake box Levi gave me, I open it and remove my father's dog tags, then smooth my thumb over the metal. It's shiny where I've touched it over the years.

I slip the chain over my head, sensing that its purpose has changed. I will always honor my father's sacrifice, but the necklace is no longer about the past. Now I wear it for another soldier, one I pray will come home to me.

My heart aches for Jess and Cole, and I wonder what the future will bring for them. For all of us. Then I hear an echo of Jess's words, and a quiet peace settles over me.

"But God."

ABOUT THE AUTHOR

Debbi Migit lives in central Illinois, surrounded by pumpkin patches and corn fields. She has won multiple awards and contests, writing stories that are filled with faith and hope. She loves to share personal anecdotes about God's faithfulness, infusing her talks with authenticity and humor.

Her first book, *Child of Promise*, is the true love story of a family formed through adoption. After ten years of infertility, Debbi and her husband, Phil, were just months from adopting when God said, "Not this way." Child of Promise is the story of audacious faith resulting in multiple miracles; it encourages readers to remember their own promises and believe again.

Debbi and Phil are the adoptive parents of Alex, Ethan, and Kate. The God-ordained spacing of their children offered the unique opportunity to parent a teen and two toddlers at the same time. This is the season Debbi fondly calls the TNT years!

Debbi's hobbies include reading, writing, and avoiding arithmetic. Her favorite color is turquoise, and she collects Trixie Belden books and typewriters. If playing Candy Crush was a paying gig, she would be rich.

Debbi's new romance/suspense series begins with *September Shadows*, and is set in Montana. After the mysterious death of their parents, three young sisters are determined to stay together and make a new life for themselves. This new life includes faith-testing danger, adventure, and romance.

MORE FROM THE JUSTICE, MONTANA SERIES

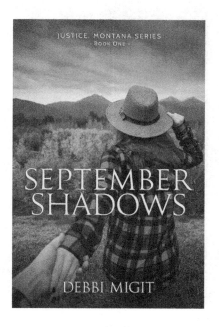

September Shadows

Book One - Justice, Montana Series

After the sudden death of their parents, Jess Thomas and her sisters, Sly and Maggie, start creating a new life for themselves. But when Sly is accused of a crime she didn't commit, the young sisters are threatened with separation through foster care. Jess is determined to prove Sly's innocence, even at the cost of her own life.

Cole McBride has been Jess's best friend since they were children. Now his feelings are deepening, just as Jess takes risks to protect her family. Can Cole convince Jess to trust him-and God-to help her?

Get your copy here:

https://scrivenings.link/septembershadows

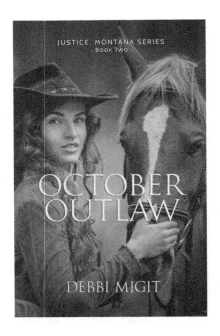

October Outlaw

Book Two - Justice, Montana Series

Two sisters. Two brothers. Two Outlaws. All headed for Justice.

Jess Thomas is being tracked by two outlaws—one is a man, and one is a beast.

When Jess uncovers new evidence concerning their parents' deaths, the Thomas sisters gain the attention of a very dangerous man. And when a cougar terrorizes Justice, Montana, Jess risks her life to save those she loves.

Cole McBride respects Jess's courage, but he fears someday she will take one risk too many.

Sly Thomas is adjusting to her new responsibilities as guardian of her two sisters. But just as she begins to hope for the future, her blossoming relationship with Deputy Nick McBride is threatened.

Get your copy here:

https://scrivenings.link/octoberoutlaw

MORE MYSTERIES FROM SCRIVENINGS PRESS

Manicures and Murder by Keri Lynn

A Texas-Sized Mystery—Book Three

When Lacey Baker's best friend is murdered only weeks before Christmas, the salon owner realizes that not all is what it seems in her small town. After an attempt is made on her own life, Lacey finds herself not only thrust back into the world of rodeo she thought she'd left behind, but also into the arms of her ex-fiancé, Cody.

With time running out, one mistake is all it will take for everything to come undone.

Get your copy here:

https://scrivenings.link/manicuresandmurder

Show Me Betrayal by Ellen E. Withers

Show Me Mysteries—Book One

Two deaths occur decades apart. Is it possible these deaths are related? What motivates a killer, who got away with murder sixty years ago, to kill again? Was it uncontrollable rage or the hope of silencing someone who fit all the puzzle pieces together and deduced who committed the crime?

Set in the picturesque town of Mexico, Missouri, *Show Me Betrayal* takes flight in words and emotions of rich characters woven together into a story you won't want to put down.

Get your copy here:

https://scrivenings.link/showmebetrayal

The Case of Misaken Identity by Deborah Sprinkle
A Mac & Sam Mystery—Book Two

Private Investigator Mackenzie Love manages to get into trouble on a simple shopping trip where she finds herself at the business end of a gun. It's clear her attacker mistakes her for someone else, but who? And why is her look-alike in so much trouble?

Mac enlists the help of her partners, Samantha Majors and Miss P, and Detective Jake Sanders to find her doppelgänger and solve the case of mistaken identity.

In the meantime, Mr. Fischer of Fischer Industries comes to the private detectives for help with a problem of his own. As Mac and Sam work on his case, they begin to wonder if the two cases are related.

Can Mac and Sam unravel the clues and get justice for both Mac's look-alike and Mr. Fischer?

Get your copy here:

https://scrivenings.link/mistakenidentity

True Blue Christmas by Susan Page Davis

True Blue Mysteries—Book Five

New neighbors, cryptic Christmas cards, and jury duty. What next? Campbell McBride is juggling her new role as a private investigator with her slightly wacky personal life. Can she and her dad figure out who stashed a valuable painting in their client's attic? And is the murder of an egocentric landlord somehow connected?

Coming November 7, 2023:

https://scrivenings.link/truebluechristmas

Made in the USA
Monee, IL
30 November 2023

47128765R00125